Extraction
Under Fire

Robert Dalcross

Published by Military Press (London)

DEDICATION

My sincere thanks to Graham A. for his tireless
assistance in the roles of military technical advisor
and finder of cloaked typos

Airborne Warrior and all-round good guy

1) Russian Naval Base, Sevastopol, Russian Occupied Crimea

Sevastopol naval base, the crown jewel of Russia's Black Sea Fleet, sprawled along the western coast of occupied Crimea. Its harbour, a five-mile finger of dark water barely a mile wide, cut eastward into the land. This strategic stronghold dominated Ukraine's maritime access, its formidable fleet effectively blockading Ukrainian naval vessels in their Odessa base.

The harbour bustled with activity. Along its North and South shores, ship berths, naval facilities, and dry docks stretched from the Marine Mammal Training Unit's guard post near the entrance. While much of the Northern shore remained undeveloped, the South teemed with industry and infrastructure.

At the harbour mouth, concrete jetties funnelled incoming vessels past a floating boom. Anti-submarine netting hung from this barrier, ready to swing open for friendly craft while barring potential intruders.

Just inside the Northern jetty, two rectangular underwater pens floated, their heavy netting descending into the murky depths. Walkways bordered the pens, and on one wider section stood a small wooden hut, its lone window casting a dim glow into the gathering dusk.

Inside this humble shelter, Starshina 1st class (Sergeant in the Russian Navy) Vasily Karpov and Starshy Matros (Corporal) Pyotr Sokolov sat ensconced in an alcohol-induced haze. Vasily, his ample belly straining against his stained uniform shirt, slurred, "Pyotr, my darling Anastasia is on duty and she has not had a drink all night!"

Pyotr stared at his friend with glassy eyes and said nothing, but in a companionable way. His skinny arms supported his head from elbows resting on their drink-wet table. Vasily stood, grasping a fresh bottle of vodka by the neck and tried to move towards the door; but instead staggered backwards into his chair. Steadying himself with his free hand on the chair-arm he leaned forward and took four unsteady steps to the door. Pyotr rose vertically to his feet and followed him out of the hut, straight-legged like a paralytic zombie.

The night air carried the tang of salt and diesel as they emerged onto the walkway. Before them stretched the dark expanse of the harbour, an abyss of secrets. Pyotr stood silent, now swaying slightly, and watched Vasily grasp a railing then lower himself to his knees. Bending awkwardly over the water on the harbour side of the pen, Vasily slapped the surface three times then rolled backwards onto the boards still clutching his bottle, holding it high with exaggerated caution. He rolled upright and looked expectantly at the black water. The inky blackness remained undisturbed. Undeterred, he tried again.

This time, as if summoned by magic, a great white head rose from the depths. The beluga whale, Anastasia, emerged, her bulbous forehead glistening in the dim light. A curious harness encircled her head, supporting a thick spike on her nose. Her massive jaws parted, revealing rows of peg-like teeth.

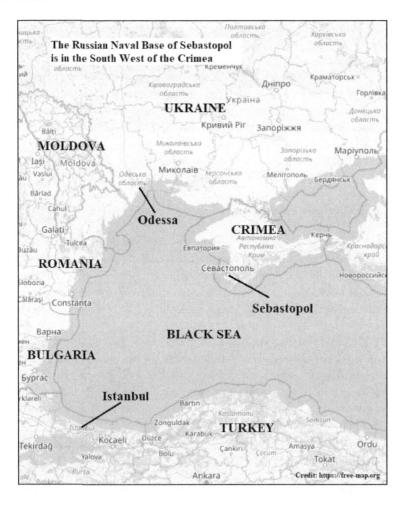

Vasily's blotchy face lit up as if he had seen his youngest child walk for the first time, "Anastasia, my darling. You drink with me?" he cooed. The Beluga whale's head moved towards and away from Vasily as she sculled; but more towards and he took this as a yes. He reached out, holding the open bottle over the open mouth, and poured in what he considered to be a generous amount of vodka for a small whale. Anastasia made a loud squeaking noise and drifted away a few yards, still with her head out of the water; then she came back again, obviously wanting more.

High above, unseen in the moonless sky, a British Watchkeeper WK450 drone silently relayed its surveillance data via satellite, confirming the absence of human activity in the open ground North of the harbour.

The harbour cradled the pride of the Russian Black Sea fleet. Three air defence frigates of the latest Admiral Gorshkov class, armed with 3M22 Zircon hypersonic cruise missiles capable of Mach 9, shared berths with attack submarines of the Kilo and 677 Lada class. Alongside these modern marvels sat older capital ships, Ivan Gren class landing ships, an assortment of tugs, service vessels, and a hospital ship. The air defence frigates stood sentinel, their advanced systems a bulwark against Ukraine's increasingly effective UAV attacks.

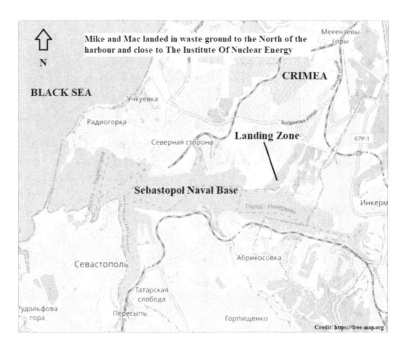

As the clock struck 03:07 on that fateful Saturday morning, two uninvited guests arrived. Silent and radar-invisible, a pair of ram-air steerable parachutes, equipment containers dangling 30 feet below, glided through the inky night sky, passing over the Institut Yadernoy Energii I Promyshlennosti. (Nuclear Energy Institute) Guided by military-grade GPS, they touched down midway along the North shore of Sevastopol harbour.

Mike Reaper, MI6 field operative and full colonel, landed first. His tall, rangy frame rolled with the impact, absorbing the shock of the uneven terrain. Close behind came Don Mac, professional Glaswegian and Sergeant in E Squadron, 22 SAS Regiment. His wiry body quick-stepped to a stand, a testament to years of covert insertions.

With practiced efficiency, they secured their parachutes, stuffing the bulky canopies into camouflaged nylon bags. From their equipment containers, Mac extracted a sleek, black torpedo-like device, roughly three feet long and six inches in diameter. He cradled it carefully, approaching the water's edge with the reverence of a priest bearing a sacred relic.

As Mac launched the device, Mike's fingers danced over the remote control unit. The torpedo's propeller whirred into life, and it slipped beneath the surface, disappearing into the harbour's depths.

Mac's eyes twinkled with feigned innocence as he turned to Mike. "Will it ken where tae go?" he asked, his thick Glaswegian accent a familiar comfort in this foreign land.

Mike smiled inwardly, appreciating Mac's well-worn act of technological scepticism. "It will patrol the harbour and keep the sea beasties away all night," he replied, playing along with the charade.

Shedding their parachute harnesses revealed dry suits beneath, a necessary barrier against the cold Black Sea waters. With meticulous care, they donned their rebreathing sets – LAR V Draeger Mark 26s – and clipped netting bags to their waists. These innocuous-looking sacks both held a dozen chunky mechanical devices, each no larger than a man's fist but carrying the potential for immense destruction.

Next came the TAC-500 Combat Swim Boards, sophisticated underwater navigation aids that would guide them through the murky depths. As the devices flickered to life, they displayed position, bearing, depth, and the direction of pre-programmed targets. Finally, they strapped on their fins, the last step in their transformation from land-based intruders to underwater wraiths.

Mac's gaze swept across the 700 yards of open water to the berthing area opposite. Three larger ships, a matched set, dominated the scene, flanked by three smaller vessels. He nodded towards the larger craft. "Them three big boats ur oor main targets, aye?"

Mike nodded, his expression grim. "Indeed they are, Mac. One is the Admiral Gorshkov, a missile frigate, and the other two are of the same class. Intel says they're equipped with the most advanced air-defence systems in the Russian arsenal. Combined with the mobile land systems, they've turned Sevastopol into an impregnable fortress against air attacks. Take those three out, and suddenly the entire fleet and dry-docks become vulnerable to Ukrainian strikes."

He gestured towards the smaller vessels. "Those are the new Vasiliy Bykov class patrol vessels. About corvette size, similar to our River Class. Sleek little devils – almost invisible to radar, and each carries a chopper on the back deck like a miniature frigate. They've been giving Ukrainian merchant ships hell lately." Mike's voice hardened. "But as Geoff emphasized at the hotel, our primary targets are those anti-air frigates. Of course," he added with a hint of dark humour, "bonus points if we can take out everything in the harbour."

Mac's response was characteristically laconic. "Aye," he grunted, the single syllable speaking volumes.

The two men waded into the dark water, their movements comically duck-like in their oversized fins. As they settled behind their DT4 Thrusters, the black water closed over their heads, leaving no trace of their presence.

Minutes later, a series of clicks echoed through the water, reaching the sensitive ears of Anastasia and her companion, Tatiana. Despite their training and the lethal CO_2 spikes mounted on their noses – capable of turning a diver into a grotesque, pizza-filled balloon – terror gripped the two beluga whales. Mistaking the sounds for a killer whale on the hunt, they abandoned their patrol route and fled to the safety of their pen, too frightened even to alert their human handlers.

As Vasily continued his drunken vigil, oblivious to the drama unfolding beneath the waves, Mike and Mac pressed on with their mission. The fate of the Black Sea Fleet – and perhaps the entire conflict – hung in the balance, dependent on the skills of these two men and the deadly cargo they carried.

2) **H.M.S. Formidable, Gulf Of Oman**
   47 Miles Off Bandar-e-Jask, Iran
   For some years Iran has been working towards developing nuclear weapons. If they had such weapons they would destabilise the economies of the entire Middle East and possibly Europe. This because they have threatened to destroy Israel and would be immune to threats of reprisal from the West for their support for various terrorist groups in the Middle East including Hezbollah in Lebanon and the Houthis in Yemen. The Houthis could potentially close the Suez canal to shipping by blocking

access to the Red Sea. An access used by 50 merchant ships a day to reach Europe from the Far East.

The Gulf of Oman is a strategic expanse of water which guards the entrance to the Persian Gulf outside the Straits of Hormuz. Iran lies to the North with Oman to the South of this busy seaway. Significantly to the events related here, all seaborne Iranian exports, such as oil, must pass through the Gulf of Oman. And Iranian oil exports are valued at about $40 Billion a year.

The British Type 31 frigate H.M.S. Formidable sliced through the clear blue waters of the Gulf of Oman with the grace of a very large cat on the prowl. Though the fuel-conserving 16 knots she was making moved air over the superstructure like a breeze, that air was scorching and the deck too hot to touch with bare skin.

Below decks her crew of 98 men and women felt like sardines in an air-conditioned can as they carried out their technical duties, cleaned ship, sweated through fire control drills and stood watch. The ship-boarding team of Royal Marines from 42 Commando worked out in the helicopter-hangar gym between bouts of exercise on the deck to harden them to the sun.

Under the Joint Comprehensive Plan of Action (JCPoA), a range of US, UN, EU and UK sanctions designed to stop Iran developing nuclear capabilities, current Iranian attempts to develop nuclear weapons were being punished by a naval blockade intended to stop the export of Iranian oil and other trade goods. A blockage enforced by US, UK, French and German warships. And the Gulf of Oman was the choke point for this operation.

All shipping from Iraq, Kuwait, United Arab Emirates and, most importantly, Iran has to pass through the Gulf of Oman to leave the Persian Gulf and make the open sea. So every ship carrying illicit Iranian oil was obliged to take this route.

Almost three weeks into her JCPoA patrol HMS Formidable had stopped more than two dozen vessels of various types suspected of trying to run the blockade against Iran. Several had been suspicious but following a search and check of their manifests, none of them had been found to be guilty of anything more than being shifty. Today, however, might be different…

Aboard Formidable, the air on the bridge became charged with tension as surface radar marked a large target. 30 miles South of Bandar-e-Jask and heading South of East at 15 knots. The only vessels of this size likely to cross their path were oil tankers. And in these waters oil tankers under any flag were a legitimate target for boarding and, if they were carrying Iranian oil, seizure.

Captain Ian Donovan, an officer well known in the service for his decision a few years ago to follow his orders to the letter yet still sink a certain blockade-running vessel, stood resolute on his bridge. Some thought he was a fine, aggressive officer, while others thought he had read too much Captain Hornblower as a boy. His gaze was fixed on the horizon but his mind was working, considering the best way to intercept and hold this potential blockade runner.

She was now formally identified as the oil tanker, Al-Qadir, an imposing Panama-flagged leviathan of something over 300,000 tonnes deadweight. A ship this size was for trans-ocean runs so she had likely loaded crude at Bandar-e Abbas and was probably en route to the Iranians' main customer, China.

But how to stop her? The fact that the Formidable weighed only 7,000 tonnes was not an issue, she bristled with guns, missiles and carried a heavily armed Wildcat helicopter. No, the problem was how to effectively "arrest" the Al-Qadir without her running back into Iranian waters, a place where even Donovan dare not go. She was only about 18 miles outside Iranian territorial waters.

If he had the Royals rope down onto the deck from the Wildcat and blow open the access doors then it turned out the cargo was legitimate he would be in serious trouble. Especially if she managed to get back across the invisible line which marked Iranian home waters.

The Formidable, as a type 31 "stealth" frigate, had a radar profile similar to that of a porpoise dorsal fin breaking the surface of the sea. She was effectively invisible to all civilian radar and most military. This is why she ran a transponder when in transit to avoid the risk of collision. On patrol the transponder was switched off so neither Al-Qadir nor Iranian coastal radar would know she was there until such times as she hailed the Al-Qadir. Unless, of course, they actually sighted her first.

"Number One," Donovan called to his first officer using the dated phrase, "Mr. Griggs, I want to get between the Al Qadir and the Iranian coast to stop her running back into their waters. Take us in an arc around the Al-Qadir to the West at a brisk pace, keeping about 20 miles distant for as far as you can, and then put us on the North side of her. Take care to keep outside the Iranian limit or they may send a flotilla of Seraj-1s out to make a scene."

"Very good sir." Lieutenant Griggs issued the appropriate orders to Navigation and the ship heeled to starboard as she turned sharply to port and increased speed from 16 to 33 knots. The bridge crew continued about their duties without a spare word but every person present was aware of what was coming.

For something to do while he waited, Donovan scanned the direction of the Al-Qadir for any kind of vessel. Nothing. Of course, the lookouts on either side of the bridge were doing the same with younger, sharper, eyes and every radar on the ship was searching the sky and sea surface for anything which might give away their position to the Iranians. Sonar, the 2093 model employing their CAPTAS-5 towed body and handling system, ceaselessly searched for underwater threats. Nothing.

One hour and 34 minutes later the watch changed but Captain Donovan and Griggs stayed on the bridge. Donovan glanced at his watch secretively. He did not want anyone to think he was anything but relaxed. He addressed the Officer of the Watch, "How long Mr. Jameson?"

"We will be in position in 7 minutes, sir. 13 miles off Iran and 15 miles North from the Al-Qadir. The sun will be behind them but they may not have seen us."

"Very good Mr. Jameson." Donovan picked up a microphone and flipped the switch, addressed the weapons officer, in his armoured operations room behind and below the bridge, "Mr. Carling, have the gun teams standing by, please."

"Yes sir."

3) **Médecins San Frontières Clinic, Huraidha**
   95 Miles North West Of Al Mukalla, Yemen,
   The queue for medical assistance ran outside the door and along the street. It wasn't just that there were no doctors locally, the important thing was that this medical assistance and this medicine was free. Everyone here was poor. Desperately poor, because anyone with money had gone to the city. And anyone here who had anything worth having had been robbed by the soldiers of one side or the other in the endless conflict.

A lot of young men liked the life of a freedom fighter. Really, they were running a protection racket. It meant you didn't have to work, you ate regular and you could take whatever you wanted from anyone who wasn't a freedom fighter. And you could settle old family scores. Sides didn't matter.

Of course that included the girls and they didn't get to say no. Well they did, but that didn't matter either.

The clinic was set up inside a house in a newish block by a couple of empty shops. The street outside was sand-strewn and empty, bar a couple of burnt out cars. Inside it was cool from the air-con and as clean as the staff could make it. It still looked like someone's house though. On the door two large Yemeni men with guns, working for MSF, let a mother with her children inside whenever the last patients left.

The clinic consisted of three doctors and three nurses, all European volunteers, and they were working flat out to slow the latest cholera epidemic. The people were all thin and hungry, which didn't help, and cholera was spreading through the children like measles. Many, many were dying and only the worst cases were being brought to the clinic. Every mother knew to make their children drink, but sometimes that wasn't enough.

The one's that came here all needed antibiotics to kill the cholera bug and they ought to get intravenous fluids to help recovery but there just wasn't time and there just wasn't the space. So they got the jabs, got the advice to get liquids down them and then they were out the door. "Next please." Its not a perfect world and this was the best they could do. But it was saving a lot of lives.

Two of the doctors were typical blond Germans, Angela and Hans, one was English, Emily Cooper. Emily was tallish, slim, dark haired and looked about 30 years of age. The skin on her face was still pale from keeping out of the sun, despite being 9 months into her 12 month posting. She waved off the girl who could not be more than 16 years old. This young mother had brought in two little boys aged 9 months and 2 years, both of whom were close to death from cholera dehydration.

A couple of jabs and some crying and they would probably both survive now. So two more lives saved. Something to feel good about. The mother was pathetically, embarrassingly grateful as Emily waved her out the door.

The next patient came in with a brood of three children, all boys. Again. "Ahlan biki, as-salam alaykum," Emily welcomed the girl and wished her peace in Arabic. And got a surprised look in return.

The mother recovered quickly and returned, "Walaykum as-salam." Polite as all Arabs are.

She was older, perhaps 18 or 20 years of age. Her face was lined with worry and she looked older than that. "Cholera," she said with a Yemeni accent, probably her only word of English. Emily checked the children for anything else that was obviously wrong, no, it looked like cholera again.

The nurse handed Emily a syringe and she popped it into the shoulder of the eldest child. He was brave and made no sound. It surely hurt the mother more.

"'Iinah shujae jdan." Emily complemented the mother on her son's bravery.

She smiled shyly. "Ant latif jidana," You are very kind.

"yatimu aliaetina' bi'atfalik jydan," Emily commented how well cared for her children looked. The girl smiled in appreciation.

Emily continued, "Hal qam alhuthiuwn bisariqat alnaas mwkhran," asking if the Houthis rebels had been robbing people in the area recently. A shadow flashed across the girl's face and her smile froze. Emily wondered if she had been clumsy. Did the girl think she was an informer?

4) **SS Al-Qadir, Gulf Of Oman**
   100 Miles Off Bandar-e-Jask, Iran
   Captain Hamza Siddiqui paced the width of his huge bridge. It took a little while as it was over 60 yards side to side. He stopped to glance at the radar screen and saw the coast of Iran around Bandar-e Jask to his North about thirty miles.
   A crewman stood behind the con but he had little to do. The officer of the watch stood by his shoulder and watched him do it. Since they had run through the straight of Hormuz and turned Eastwards their course would take them through the Gulf of Aden and well clear of Muscat, Oman to the South then down across the Arabian Sea to round Sri Lanka and then to Singapore en route for China. He looked at the Safecaptain navigation system and noted that there would not be a course correction until the next waypoint in almost three hours. Perhaps a coffee was in order?

He pulled out his wallet and looked at the photo of his wife, Mishti and their little family. In his mind he was back home in their garden with his family around him. It would be his eldest son's birthday tomorrow and Waqas would be 8 years old. "How quickly time flies," he thought. Then considered how long it was since he last saw his family in Chandpur, Bangladesh. Not to worry, just another 7 months and he would be home again. And he would be bringing presents for his wife and presents for his children and presents for his parents. Life was good.

Hamza's reverie was shattered by a stern call over Channel 16, the VHF hailing frequency. "Al-Qadir, Al-Qadir, Al-Qadir, this is His Majesty's Frigate Formidable. Do you copy, over?"

Hamza's eyes opened wide and he dropped his wallet. But he knew what to do. He called to the officer of the watch, for the ears of the crewman on the con, "Hard a Port, engines to full speed. We must get into Iranian waters before we are boarded!"

The level of noise from the engines far below raised a little but nothing else could be seen or felt as the huge ship began its turn and acceleration.

The screen for the stern camera showed the wash from the propellers increasing and the ship was coming out of the line drawn by its own wash as it did begin to turn.

"Al-Qadir, Al-Qadir, Al-Qadir, this is His Majesty's Frigate Formidable. I am sending a boarding party by helicopter to check your manifest. Maintain your previous course. Do not turn to the North. I repeat, do not turn to the North, over."

Hamza stroked where his beard would be and addressed the officer of the watch, "Usman, continue the turn and get us into safe waters," he strode over to the radar screen, "Where is that warship?"

Seeing nothing on radar he automatically scanned the horizon with his eyes, then snatched up a pair of powerful binoculars and peered through those. The lookouts on either end of the bridge were already doing the same. They called in to the officer of the watch, "Nothing sighted, sir."

The ship was half turned towards the Iranian shore now and something appeared on the port bow at the edge of visibility. They were staring into the sun and there was a mist over the calm water. The port lookout called out, "Sir, a ship, looks like a warship."

The Al-Qadir was actually turning to approach their interrogator. Hamza's jaw dropped.

The officer of the watch saw the threat and addressed his captain, "What should I do sir?"

"Continue the manoeuvre, we will sail right past them, they cannot stop us Usman."

A moment after he spoke two high explosive "smart" shells from a Bofors 57mm Mark 110 gun exploded in the air either side of the bridge. The toughened sea-glass on the starboard wing cracked, either under the shockwave or from a piece of shrapnel.

The VHF spoke again, ""Al-Qadir, Al-Qadir, Al-Qadir, this is His Majesty's Frigate Formidable. I am sending a boarding party by helicopter to check your manifest. Return to your previous course. Cancel your turn to the North. I repeat, do not turn to the North. If you do not comply I will target your bridge, over."

High overhead, and coming out of the sun, Hamza could now see a rather fierce looking helicopter approaching them. Had he been more knowledgeable about the Royal Navy he would have known it to be an AgustaWestland AW159 Wildcat carrying a disciplined but very aggressive boarding team from J Company, 42 Commando, Royal Marines.

Hamza threw up his hands in a rather theatrical, Middle-Eastern display of despair and took the VHF microphone, "Formidable, Formidable, Formidable, this is Al-Qadir. I will comply with your orders. Please do not fire again, over."

5) **Russian Naval Base, Sevastopol**
Russian Occupied Crimea, Ukraine
The Volkswagen taxi stopped for no obvious reason where the access road to the university ran through the waste land a few hundred yards from the harbour. Mike and Mac jumped up from the hedge and into the car which moved off quickly. The driver, wearing a grey track suit and blue woolly hat, said nothing for a while then, "You English?"

Mike assumed he was Ukrainian and replied, "My brytantsi. Ty smilyva lyudyna, shcho robysh tse." We are British. You are a brave man doing this.

The man shook his head, "Your Ukrainian is pretty good. I do speak English. I am just a patriot. My name is Pavlo."

"Good to know you Pavlo, My name is Mike. Do you have the clothes for us?"

"Civilians clothes in boot of car. Papers too. To show you as officer and your partner as sergeant. As ordered by London. You will have less trouble that way if you are stopped."

Mac snorted quietly.

"Ideal. How far is it to the Brotherhood Cemetery?"

"It is only 5 minutes direct but on our way there is a place of garages on Bohdanova Street where you can change privately."

"Sounds good."

The car picked up speed as it reached Bohdanova Street and in a few seconds pulled off into a network of garages. Many had small chimneys and appeared to be lived it. It pulled up opposite one garage much like another, "You are safe here, they are friends. Follow me."
Pavlo took bags from the car boot and led them inside. It was a garage turned into a kind of bedsit. "Change here."

Mike and Mac changed out of their dry suits and put on the old-fashioned clothing provided. "I guess this is what the well dressed Russian officer wears off duty?" Mike spoke lightly.

"It is so," Pavlo was not up to the subtleties of British Army humour, "Here are ID cards and papers. Put radios and kit in bags." Pavlo led them back to the car and they set off again.

Two minutes later he pulled into an ornate gateway marked, "Bratskoye kladbishche," in Russian. The Brotherhood Cemetery. Early as it was, the car park was empty and there was just an old man walking an old dog amongst the trees.

Pavlo nodded at an ornate stone pyramid some 55 feet tall in the centre of the cemetery. It had the look of a megalithic monument to some alien god but in reality it was Saint Nicholas' Church. There was a cross at the peak and some type of belfry below that. Lower down, there were dormer windows then more extended versions along each side.

"Wow!" Mike exclaimed, "It is more impressive in reality than the picture."

"Fur fox sake!" Mac had just caught sight of the amazing structure.

"It is a chapel of the Russian Orthodox Church," Pavlo said, matter-of-factly. "127,000 Russian soldiers were buried here after you and the French beat them in 1854. They hold it as a kind of memorial. The Russians like to celebrate their own deaths."

"I guess we Brits do too. Do you have the keys?"

"Yes, I will show in and lock up when you installed. It is used not often, only some anniversaries. It should be safe for few days. I will hide keys to your room." Pavlo walked towards the chapel and the two men followed.

"How do you want us to contact you."

"Best you call London. They relay message to my people."

"Fine."

Pavlo unlocked the old door with an over-large key. The interior was decorated with beautiful religious frescoes and dark carved wood. He led them up some narrow, wooden stairs to an upper room, perhaps a vestry, and then further up again

through a trap-door to a type of belfry containing just one large bell. A small square room perhaps 20 feet on a side with a dark bronze bell hanging in the middle and ropes to control it. One each wall, an opening to let the sound of the bell out and the wind in.

"There are intercept units here. Try keep radio message short."

Mike smiled and nodded, "Of course," But he knew their comms system would focus upwards towards a certain satellite and be untraceable.

Pavlo was standing awkwardly. "It was good meet allies for first time Mike." He smiled briefly and extended a hand to shake.

Mike took the hand and shook it warmly, "It was good to meet you too Pavlo. I wish you the best of luck in all that you do. Take good care of yourself."

Pavlo smiled more confidently and showed a black tooth. He nodded to Mac and shook his hand then climbed back down through the trap-door and they heard it lock beneath their feet.

When he was safely out of earshot Mac shared his opinion, ""This is a pure rubbish hideout."

"I know Mac. It's the highest place for many miles around and if I suspected there was a spy watching the naval base it is the first place I would look."

"Aye."

"But we don't have any choice in the matter do we? So let's just hope we get a signal from intel in short order."

6) Sir Henry Attwood's Office
Whitehall, London

Whitehall is just a road in the centre of London, but it is a rather spectacular road as its name might suggest. It is lined by a great many fine buildings, amongst which are a royal palace and a number of important government offices. Due to the presence of so many government office buildings full of civil servants, the name of the road is very often used to refer to UK government administration as a whole.

The grandeur of Whitehall, steeped in some hundreds of years of history and reeking of power, served as a suitable setting for the office of self-styled Whitehall mandarin, Sir Henry Attwood. Certainly, he thought so.

Sir Henry's office might have been a film set for a movie set in nineteenth century Britain and doubtless featuring gun-boat diplomacy. Carved oak panels covered the walls below the dado rail and paintings by masters, borrowed by government from national institutions, were arranged above it in understated splendour where they would not detract from Sir Henry's photographic records of his own, not insubstantial, achievements in the world of diplomacy.

Photographs mostly from his younger days before his temples showed a distinguished grey and his waist-coat became a little tight around the middle from too little early morning squash and too many late night dinners.

Henry was head of the entire British SIS; the Secret Intelligence Service. An organisation comprising MI5 for threats within the UK, MI6 for foreign threats or foreign action, GCHQ for signals and several other less well known units.

He was answerable only to the most senior of the several government Ministers in charge of the entire Foreign Office. And then only nominally because Ministers, while appointed by the Prime Minister to oversee government departments, are unable to learn the workings of a huge organisation overnight, if ever.

For this reason Ministers must rely on civil servants to run the day-to-day business of their charge and while doing so make most of the tactical decisions. And this gives civil servants at this exalted level a great deal of power. As it ought, in all fairness, given the ability of some elected politicians. At least civil servants are selected and promoted by ability. Sadly, neither their politics nor their loyalty is ever questioned.

There was a polite tap on Sir Henry's door and Chief Intelligence Officer Ralf Burgin, SIS, walked in, smiling grimly at his almost-friend as he crossed the floor and positioned himself ready to sit opposite Sir Henry with some familiarity. Ralf was a wiry man with a Roman nose and a way of moving his head which reminded some people of a bird. Those few who knew him better than others tended to think of a raptor. Perhaps a peregrine falcon but more a merlin from the immaculate, slate blue jacket he so often wore.

"Ah, good morning Ralf. How are you?" Henry pressed a discrete button under the edge of his desk.

"Mustn't grumble my friend," Ralf had the subtle air of one going through the motions of friendship. They shook hands over the desk and Ralf sat down.

"Did you hear our people have taken an oil tanker running the Iran blockade?"

"Signal came through last night. Neat little op from what I hear."

"Seems so," Henry's patrician dismissal of lesser mortals was apparent to Ralf's tuned ear, "It is en route for Diego Garcia, British Indian Ocean Territories, as we speak. A 320,000 tonne tanker full of crude impounded is a significant loss to Iran. And doubtless their top brass are like wet hens."

"I am sure they are. I am sure they are Henry. China is not known for its charity and if they do not deliver their oil then China will delay delivery of their nuclear and weapons technology. What do you think the Iranians will do?"

A smiling, respectful young lady put her head around the door and took Henry's order for tea and biscuits before he continued, "They have no shortage of oil but they are struggling to get it to China. Between us and the French we are stopping more ships than get through. I think they will kick up a diplomatic fuss, claiming some kind of loophole whereby it should not be stopped. And when that doesn't work they will do something to embarrass us."

"I see where you are coming from but I think they will move straight to trying to embarrass us, put pressure to release the ship."

A keen observer might have noticed a tell in Henry's voice in response to the subtle change in the balance of status now reflected in their conversation, "And do you have any idea what that might be Ralf?"

"Not without I find a crystal ball, Henry." Ralf back-tracked almost indiscernibly. Almost.

"They have used Hezbollah in Lebanon before now." Henry was guessing to recover the initiative.

"True, but I think that would be too indirect. We could ignore anything *they* get up to. They will try something to harm us directly I think."

"Probably a bombing or a kidnapping then." Henry was comfortable in his status once more.
"I think that is most likely. But we can do very little or nothing about either until they happen, aside from the obvious precautions, so we must just sit tight and wait."

Henry dropped on the opportunity to emphasise his power like a cat with a captive mouse, "Then perhaps it would be a good idea to have your people ready to respond to a kidnapping?"

Ralf was ready for him, "Of course you are right Henry, but you know how stretched we are with the last round of budget cuts. I have Reaper on a job that a junior MI6 operator ought to be doing. So I can pull him out and onto this if it turns out to be something we can influence. I do understand your concerns."

The door opened, the men stopped talking, and the same young lady entered; all smiles and a subtle, rather pleasant, perfume blending with the scent of Earl Gray tea.

7) **General Fazad's Office, Khatam-al Anbiya**
   Iranian Army Central Headquarters, Tehran, Iran
   The Khatam al-Anbiya Central Headquarters was the unified combatant command headquarters of the Iranian Armed Forces, which faceless unit came under the direct command of the General Staff.

Built in 2016, the main building was a rather pleasing tower block of 14 stories faced in sand-coloured concrete. Somewhat longer than it was wide, the ends were rounded in a graceful curve. Doubtless by chance, the headquarters buildings stood amongst a collection of others which included the Erfan Hospital, the Bahman Hospital, the Atieh Hospital and the Laleh Hospital.

The commanding officer of this institution was Major General Gholam Fazad, a sharp-eyed, broad, moustachioed individual, whose belly had increased along with his rank. Originally from the Quds Force, the elite clandestine wing of Iran's Islamic Revolutionary Guard Corps, he was now responsible for all manner of operations both foreign and domestic which the government of Iran would rather not acknowledge publically.

His office enjoyed a view from the top floor of the block and across the busy, attractive city of Tehran. A view which sported more modern buildings and greenery than some might expect. On this day, however, General Fazad was not admiring the view. He was venting his frustration at Special Forces Colonel Amir Tehrani, a tall, fit looking man of perhaps 35 years who sported a scar across his left cheek. The Colonel remained at attention while the world situation, and particularly that part of it relating to Special Forces, was explained to him.

General Fazad stood behind his desk and leaned forward onto his straight arms, planted upon it. "…and that is why I sent for you, Colonel. Someone very high in the religious community has asked me to resolve this theft of the Al-Qadir and I immediately thought of you.

"Thank you sir."

"Thank you sir?" Fazad was exasperated at his own politically awkward position, not at the keen young Colonel whom he actually quite admired, "You may not be thanking me when you know what I require of you. It is nothing daring or heroic such as might win you a medal or a mention in the news.

I want you to have your tame Houthis in Yemen take me a hostage. A British hostage whom we can hold, claim the kidnap is an independent act of the Houthis, and then offer to intercede for if the British release our tanker. Do you like the sound of that?"

"Sir, I can think of nothing else we can do. It is not the act of a warrior to take a hostage but we must all get our hands dirty if necessary for the greater good of Iran and the revolution."

The General shook his head at the word-perfect response from an officer who was going to go a long way.

8) RAF RC-135 Airseeker, 45,000 feet
50 Miles South Of Sevastopol, Russian Naval Base

The Boeing RC-135 Airseeker, otherwise known as the Rivet Joint, was the updated, uprated version of the old RC-135 used by the US Air Force since 1962 to collect signals intelligence around the world. The airframe had remained pretty much the same but the engines were newer, more economical for longer range, and the signals kit has been uprated to something from Star Wars.

Imagine a four-engine, 130 tonne airliner full of electronic gadgets and 30 or so technical specialists. An airliner that can loiter for more than 8 hours listening in to every enemy conversation live, as it happens. And then can refuel on the wing and do it again.

The task in life of the Airseeker is to loiter over or close to a specific area of interest and soak up all the radar, radio, internet, telephone and wire traffic that is transmitted by anyone and anything in that area.

How they do this is, of course, highly classified and highly technical. What is even more puzzling is how they can listen to several thousand conversations over various types of media, all in foreign languages and all at once. But then, it is technical.

The mission of this particular RC-135, on this particular day, was to hang around the Northern part of the Black Sea and listen to every whisper taking place within Sevastopol naval base.

From these almost countless, mostly unrelated, mostly boring conversations, the artificial intelligence onboard was able to discern patterns and forecast the movement of shipping with very acceptable accuracy.

A green light began to flash, one of many such lights on a framework supporting radar and computer screens. "Sir, I have a green light on the Ladnyy, Guided Missile Frigate. She is approaching Sevastopol at 16 knots from the South and is at 43 miles distance. I have an ETA of 2 hours and 10 minutes at this speed."

"Copy that (I hear you) Sergeant, tell me if there is any change of speed or course such as might suggest a change in intention. Corporal Wallis, patch that data through to base."

"Wilco, sir." (I will comply with your order)

"Wilco, sir.

9) Saint Nicholas Church, Brotherhood Cemetery
Sevastopol, Russian Occupied Crimea, Ukraine

In the belfry there was a decorated, but open, window-like hole on each wall, almost certainly to allow the faithful to hear the bell more clearly. The holes also let in the wind which was neither warm nor inconsiderable when it blew off the sea and up the gentle hill from the harbour. Mac was curled up in a sleeping bag with an appropriate balaclava woollen helmet covering his entire head. He appeared to be asleep. Mike shook his head, three days into this OP and Mac had made himself at home.

Mike was wrapped in a blanket over his combats and staring through binoculars at the entrance to the harbour. A great many security lights meant he could see his target clearly. To keep awake he checked every few minutes to ensure it was not open for shipping. He glanced at his watch, 05:23, it would be light soon. Looking over to Mac he saw a man asleep on his back with a Glock 17 by his head and a yard-long tube with aiming sights and some wire extending from one end.

In the far corner there was a satellite phone system with a tiny dish pointing up towards the roof. Their covert communications with London via a military satellite. A blue light flashed on the phone, a call was coming in. Mike got up from his position and stretched his cold, stiff limbs then ducked and shuffled over to the phone. Picking up the handset he pressed the silent-mode to answer the call. On a small screen a text message lit up.

"Ladnyy, Guided Missile Frigate approaching Sevastopol. ETA approximately 17 minutes."

Pressing the appropriate button with his left hand and typing with his right Mike tapped out his reply, "Copy that. All good." Then he put down the phone, turned to Mac and shook his foot carefully at arms length. Entirely failing to disappoint him, Mac jerked instantly into a waking state and his pistol was up and levelled before he took a breath.

"Steady, Buddy, we have a ship coming in to harbour in 15 minutes."

"Ah, fine." Mac chose not to waste words but sat up and inspected the tube. On closer inspection it was a series of short rods fitted together to make a longer length. He twisted the connections to check their tightness. The wires at the end were a couple of yards long and led to a small box. At the end where these connected to the rod, there was something which looked like a trigger. Mac picked up the tube and attached box and carried the entire apparatus gently to the window Mike had used to watch the harbour entrance.

"Ye ever used one o' these afore?" Mac indicated the tube with a dip of his head.

"Only in training, and that only on land."

"They're pure guid but ah've only used them oan land an' aw."

Mike checked his watch.

"The boat's here."

"Go ahead and light up the buoy. The boom and nets will have to open for the frigate any minute now."

"Right ye are." Mac sighted along the tube at something in the water a hundred yards off the outside of the harbour wall by the entrance. He pressed the trigger and a red light behind the trigger turned green.

"Did you get it?"

"Ah reckon. Must have." Mac repeated the action. "Light turned green."

"Well, we will just have to trust the tech as they say."

"Who th' Fuck says tha'?"

Mike smiled to himself. "I think the light turning green means the target replied it had been triggered. But it either works or it doesn't. You will have hit the buoy with the laser and its sonar message either triggered the beacons under the ships or it didn't."

The frigate Ladnyy was heading for the harbour entrance now. She was about a hundred yards short. The gates *must* be open.
"Whaur ur the bloody Ukrainians hidin'?"

"No idea, mate, no idea."

No sooner had he spoke than the three frigates which formed their main target were almost lifted out of the water one after the other by huge explosions, their backs clearly broken. A split second later another three blasts under other vessels, then more and more until almost every ship in the harbour was destroyed. Flames lit up the wrecked vessels and the black smoke of burning fuel oil spread across the water.

"A man's goat tae be careful who he opens the door tae."

Without a word, Mac quickly, deftly packed their kit. Mike typed, "Busker, Reaper, Sunrise" on the satellite phone to call in the result. Then he pressed send.

10) Médecins San Frontières Clinic, Huraidha
95 Miles North West Of Al Mukalla, Yemen

Bilal wiped some dust from the top-cover of his AK47 and lifted his feet off the floor alternately to get the blood flowing. It was a boring job guarding the medical clinic, and it made him a bit of an outcast with some of his relatives, but it was a job, that rare prize. And it fed his family, the only important thing. It was early afternoon and the queue had shrunk down from almost 100 to now 7 women with their children. They all looked tense and quiet. He caught Saad's eye and indicated the queue with his head. Saad shook his head. Something was not right.

Bilal turned and stepped inside the door to see Dr Emily applying dressings as fast as she could work on a small child. She'd had the skin burnt off her face and upper body from an accident with cooking oil. "Asbahat qayimat aliantizar qasiratan. hunak shay ghayr sahihin." The queue has grown short, something is wrong.

Emily looked up, frustration on her face, "la yumkinuna 'iighlaq aleiadat fi kuli marat yasmae fiha alsukaan almahaliyuwn shayieatan. 'abq 'aeyunik maftuha." We cannot close the clinic every time the locals hear a rumour. Keep your eyes open. She had noticed two of the nurses had not arrived for work today.

Bilal nodded, "Naeam duktur." Yes Doctor. Outside, he caught Saad's questioning eye and shook his head, "rubama la shay.' Probably nothing.

Just as he spoke a heavy-looking woman walked around the corner of the block and came into his view at a distance of about ten feet. She was wearing the black abaya and veil which were becoming popular now amongst women who did not want to be harassed by the zealots. He looked away, as was polite.

It would have made no difference whatever he had done as the woman pressed a button held in her right hand and detonated the explosive jacket she was wearing under her abaya. The blast cut her in two and sent he upper body shooting skywards.

The explosive charges were surrounded by nuts and bolts to act as shrapnel and these tore outwards in all directions.

They swept mangled bodies of Bilal and Saad towards the queue of women and children then took these too and spread the blood and torn bodies along the road.

Then… nothing. No one ran out into the street, no screams, no sirens or alarms went off. The street remained eerily quiet. For a few moments. Then a large Nissan car swept around the corner and four armed men jumped out. One remained on the street, in the doorway to the clinic with his AK47 at the ready, the others ran inside.

Fortunately, there were no street-facing windows in the room where Emily worked so she was spared the flying glass, the usual accompaniment to street bombs in the West. But the blast-wave had stunned her and she was leaning against a work-surface. The mother clutched her screaming child, a futile reaction to her instinctual drive to keep him safe. The first man into the room called, "Doctor," and Emily turned her head to him. He pointed her out to his companions and they grabbed her by the shoulders and led her from the room and outside.

The leader of the kidnap team stepped out onto the street first. He looked left and right for threats and saw none, his swarthy face a mask devoid of any humanity. His men bundled Emily into the car and with a last look around he climbed into the front passenger seat and the vehicle drove away leaving a cloud of diesel smoke behind it.

11) The Convent, Gibraltar

It was 21:16 when the Battenberg pattern police pick-up stopped outside the Convent and opposite the white stone portico which extended out from the imposing brick building proper. The residence of the British Governor of Gibraltar since 1728. A rather sweaty Royal Navy Lieutenant, Andrew Johnson, climbed out of the passenger door and stepped around the vehicle towards the portico waving his thanks to his friend, a rather cheerful looking Gibraltar Police officer, as he did so.

Johnson was wearing mess dress with his cap so the two guards stationed under the portico came up to attention and presented arms in salute. Johnson returned the salute as he walked in. He was met in the foyer by an older man in civilian black-tie with the bearing of a maître d'. "I need to see Commodore Lewis," he said; gave his name and received a nod in response. The man scuttled off and through a rather grand, carved door.

The Governor's banqueting hall was perhaps 50 feet long and 25 feet to the apex of the ornate, pitched-beam ceiling. The beams were almost hidden by the array of flags and shields displaying a plethora of knightly ranks and orders. On the walls were oil paintings of past governors and other worthy individuals from centuries past.

The dining table was set for 14 of Gibraltar's "great and good", both military and civilian; and the diners were arrange male by female along each side according to proper usage. The maitre d'-type arrived silently by the right shoulder of Commodore Lewis and awaited an end to the conversation he was suffering with a heavy, rather overdressed woman sporting a red face.

The Commodore turned and raised a querying eyebrow to the maitre d' who bent to whisper, "Sir, there is an officer asking for you."

A flash of understanding, and perhaps relief, crossed the Commodore's face and he rose, made his excuses to the ladies on either side and followed the maitre d' out of the room.

In the foyer Johnson came up to attention and saluted his boss. The Commodore returned the salute, perfunctorily and raised an eyebrow in query.

"Sir, you asked me to report the moment our people on Diego Garcia had sight of Al-Qadir and she is about 10 miles from her berth now, accompanied, as you ordered, by HMS Diamond."

"Thank you Lieutenant. I am assuming there is a naval crew aboard Al-Qadir?"

"Yes sir. 30 of our people were flown out from Portsmouth via Oman and a fresh contingent of Royals put aboard. The civilian crew will be back in Bangladesh by now and the Captain and his officers are still on board. I understand they are under open arrest and quite friendly with the Royals."

"Mmm. Very good. I am assuming the US will be handling the tanker's security?"

Johnson nodded, "Sir."

"Fine chaps and competent but I would like them to have the support of our intel people and the SBS unit on station. The Iranians could try just about anything and I don't want an incident with the Al-Qadir on my watch."

"I will sort that out, sir."

"Can I get back to my dinner now, Lieutenant?"

12) The King's Private Office, Buckingham Palace, London, UK

His Majesty, King Charles III sat at an antique wooden desk with a slightly worn, green leather top, its rich mahogany frame gleaming under the warm light from a pattern-leaded window. A chessboard was spread out in front of him, the scattered pieces telling a tale of a recently concluded game. This was a man who relished careful strategy, not just in games, but in the very stewardship of his kingdom.

There was a polite tap at the door and a livered footman opened it to usher in a middle-aged man sporting immaculate morning dress. A man who looked like a professor from one of the better universities. Perhaps Edinburgh or Cambridge.

"Rupert," the King began, "I trust you had a pleasant trip up here?"

Sir Rupert Greville was the King's Spymaster, a man whose remarkable attributes would embarrass him, were they ever spoken of. He had served the King, and before him his mother, for decades in a number of posts relating to diplomacy and intelligence, rising eventually to head the shadowy intelligence organisation, referred to only as the Palace Security Group. A name carefully chosen to give the impression of a group of uniformed veterans guarding palaces.

This organisation, the PSG, stood above and behind the avowed agencies which openly protected the nation's security, such as the SIS. In reality, it was the instrument through which the King watched over his people and made adjustments behind the scenes where necessary. The reader might not be surprised to hear that a great many loyal and honourable people reported to the King about matters regarding which they had specialist knowledge or access.

It went without saying that Sir Rupert was a man of impeccable character and unfaltering loyalty to the crown; but he also had the brain of a maths professor, an eidetic memory and a knowledge of political matters which rivalled even that of the King.

"Thank you, sir," Rupert replied. He was not a man for small talk and his eyebrows asked permission to begin the briefing.

The King noticed and half smiled to himself. "When you are ready Rupert. I will have your favourite tea sent in." The King touched a discrete button but looked to Rupert.

"The young lady… doctor who was taken hostage by the Houthi faction recently is in the process of becoming a bargaining chip for the Iranians. I thought you might have taken a view and have instructions for me.

"Is the SIS aware of this yet, Rupert?"

"They will be by now, sir."

"Are we agreed that this poor young lady will likely be the first in a series of embarrassments to the government if the Iranians are allowed to gain their point here?"

"We are, sir."

"Then if the SIS choose to rescue her, lend whatever aid we may. If they do not so choose then have one of our people exert sufficient influence in that direction. And swiftly before the situation escalates. Do you have any comment?"

"I think that is probably our wisest course, sir. Before she is transported to an Iranian prison would be the most straightforward option. I would suggest we have Colonel Reaper assigned to this mission."

"Reaper? Very good, sir. And his Scottish… associate?"

"I think that goes without saying."

A look of distaste flickered across Rupert's face and was instantly gone.

The King did not miss it and smiled inside. "Then make it so please, Rupert."

13) Sir Henry Attwood's Office, Whitehall, London
The smiling young lady brought Henry's order of tea and biscuits and placed it between himself and Ralf. She left like a mouse and they watched her go, a constraint on their conversation in two ways.

" So, the other shoe has dropped," Ralf stated the obvious to restart the discussion where it had paused.

"Indeed it has. But we cannot say the tactic was a surprise. Merely that they were so quick off the mark."

"I should think they had this as a contingency plan in case of another tanker seizure or event of a similar nature."

"Probably so, Ralf. And I am assuming you are similarly prepared to deal with it?"

Ralf smiled, "Well you did give me a warning order… As we discussed, I kept an eye on what we were giving Reaper so we could pull him out of Ukraine and onto this job at short notice."

"This job? What are you up to?" Henry smiled but betrayed just the smallest sign of displeasure that Ralf should already have a plan underway without his authority.

"I was going to call you today anyway and get your authority for a rescue operation."

Mollified, Henry relaxed in his chair. He stirred his tea as he thought. "Our priority is to avoid the government being placed in a situation where they are shown by the press to be stuck between holding the tanker and getting Doctor Cooper released. Whichever choice they made would be wrong. You go ahead, put Reaper in theatre, release or eliminate Dr Cooper and keep me informed of developments."

Ralf placed his cup carefully back onto its saucer, "I will do just that, Henry."

"Is that Scottish person still with him?"

"I am afraid he is, Henry."

"For my life, I do not know how an officer can tolerate that insubordinate creature."

"No, Henry, it is rather strange." As Henry sipped his tea, the right edge of Ralf's mouth turned up in a smile.

14) Shallowbrook Farm, Near Horsham, Sussex, UK

Dan shut the door of his Land Rover and stood for a moment looking across the valley at his farm; he had almost doubled its size since his father retired. He had diversified into making ice cream, rather than almost giving the milk to the supermarkets and now he was making sausages like his mother used to, but by the hundred thousand. He turned to his house and opened the door to the kitchen.

Inside the warm, well lit kitchen his wife Penny was tending the Aga; she tasted a stew of some kind and added a little paprika. Dan stepped in with his socks half off his feet, having left his wellies in the porch. He glanced up at the chatter from a TV nailed high on the wall. Penny smiled, a look of contentment on her well-worn face. "What did the vet say, Darling?"

"Had to do a Caesar on the mare but mother and foal are fine."

"Oh, I am glad. Emily would have been devastated if anything happened to Poppy."

The tone of the news turned even more serious as a plastic-faced clone announced a fresh article, "…this evening that a British Doctor, Emily Cooper, has been kidnapped by Houthis Rebels in Yemen yesterday."

The couple turned to the screen, Penny's face frozen, Dan's jaw dropped.

"Iran has denounced the kidnapping and offered to assist in negotiations for the Doctor's release on condition that the British Government release the illegally detained oil tanker Al-Qadir currently in British hands at Diego Garcia."

Penny's hands flew to her face. She turned to Dan Cooper and he held her.

15) <u>Tuesday 06:35</u> Nemo Hotel, Odesa, Ukraine

Mike and Mac shared a twin room, as usual when on operations. But this room was a lot better than the average. The Nemo hotel was a 4 star outfit with en suite facilities, a drawing room and a balcony overlooking the harbour. Two friendly Ukrainian girls had joined them in the bar last night and stayed over. Mac was giving his new, and apparently rather excitable, friend a final, energetic seeing-to before breakfast.

Mike watched him across the sleeping body of his new friend. A rather lovely blond girl of perhaps 25 years who went by the name of Alina and had recently qualified as a dentist. She had nice teeth, too. The Garmin satellite phone on his bedside table shook and emitted an agreeable buzz. Mike reached over Alina and put the phone to his ear. He could use voice when off ops.

Ralf's voice spoke to him, "I have a nice little job for you in the warm, Mike."

Mike replied with good natured sarcasm, "Oh, excellent, I do like the warm. Walls and ears Ralf."

"Copy that. Did you hear about the British Doctor kidnapped in Yemen the other day?"

"No, I was on ops." Mike's tone shared a less-than-subtle humour.

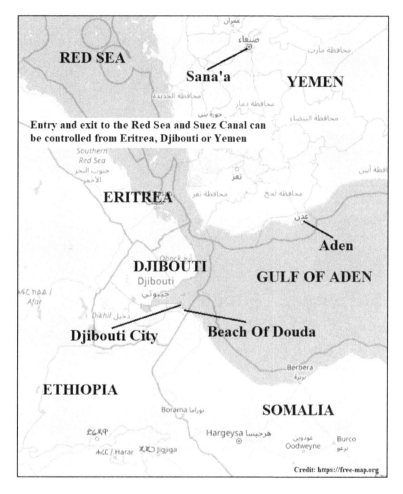

"A girl working for Medecin San Frontier was taken, apparently by the Houthis. But the Iranians pull their strings. Government desperately wants her released or eliminated before she is shipped off to Iran and used as a bargaining counter. And you are in the barrel. I have put together the quickest trip into theatre that I can at short notice."

"Fair enough. What's the plan?"

"You and Mac turn up in civvies with your toothbrushes, and absolutely no mil-kit, on the hard-standing by the loading berth on the seaward side of the oil tanks."

"Opposite the Chinese Consul's outfit?"

"… That's the place. Turn up there in 45 minutes and a Merlin will take you to Istanbul Airport. I will send the full briefing by email and you can read it en route."

"Sounds good. Tell the chopper crew to call Reaper on VHF channel 16 as they make their approach."

"Wilco Mike. Have a good trip."

16) <u>Tuesday 08:53</u> Merlin HC4a Helicopter
North Of Istanbul, Black Sea

A Merlin HC4a from the destroyer HMS Dauntless had picked them up as advertised and was now well into the 380 mile trip to Istanbul Airport.

Mac was looking at an app on his issue mobile phone, "He's goat his toe doon, the pilot. 181 miles per hour he's daein'."

"Ralf will have told him we have a civvy flight to catch in Istanbul."

"Twat." Mac had no time for Ralf.

"We'll be there inside the hour and make the flight easy, I should think."

"Aye. Ye ever been tae Djibouti afore?"

"No, never. Nice place is it?" Mike knew what was coming.

"I hear it's a shite-hole. A pal wis posted there wi' the French Foreign Legion. Para, Second Rep. Sand, shite, an' flies is aw."

"The flight from Istanbul to Djibouti is just under 6 hours. And I expect we won't be in Djibouti more than an hour or two."

"Guid."

17) Prisoner's Tent, Houthis Camp, Seiyun
Hadhramaut Valley, Yemen

The canvas of the tent was somewhere between olive drab and dark-sand so it had probably been military issue once. It was roughly circular and about 20 feet across with a pole in the centre supporting the roof. Currently, the pole also restrained Emily from moving very far from where she stood because her hands were fastened at the wrist, behind her back and on the other side of the pole.

There were two women with a collection of 5 small children between them huddled against the wall of the tent. It was not obvious if they were prisoners or guests as they would not reply to Emily's questions. The women just stared, the children occasionally cried. They all looked weak and unhappy so they were probably not part of the Houthis group. Probably.

The man who had led the kidnap team stepped into the tent and swaggered across to Emily. He was a little taller than she was and slim; perhaps 35 years old and rather attractive in a swarthy sort of way. He looked stereotypically Arab with his military fatigues and red and white kaffiyeh headdress secured with a black Agal ring. At his belt he had an automatic pistol in an enclosed holster, to keep out the sand, and the curved Jambiya knife worn by most Arab men to display their cultural heritage.

He stopped close enough to Emily's face to show he had no concept of social distancing or personal space. Close enough also to choke her with his halitosis. She restrained the urge to knee him in the groin and looked down, modestly.

"I am Rashid-Malik al-Houthi, leader of all Houthis," he proclaimed in English, as if this were a matter of great significance. He placed his fingers under Emily's chin and lifted her face to see her eyes. She looked down.

"You are a spy for the British and you will be taken to Iran and tortured until you confess." He seemed quite pleased at this prospect. Emily said nothing and kept her eyes down so far as she could.

18) <u>Tuesday 18:44</u> Djibouti International Airport
Djibouti, Gulf Of Aden

It was getting dark as Mike and Mac escaped the air-conditioning-free baggage hall of Djibouti International Airport for the slightly cooler air outside. They stepped out from under the tall colonnades supporting a portico in front of the main doors navigated the pedestrian crossing, taking extreme care. Traffic in Djibouti takes no prisoners.

"There's a Pizza Hut around the corner Mac."

Mac gave him a sidelong look which, by Mike's reading, suggested the food would be disgusting and he, Mike, crazy for eating it.

"I didn't have you down as a fussy eater." Mike looked away to maintain the craic.

"Well, Ah could dae wi' a bite masel.'"

Ten minutes later they had eaten half a decent pizza each to take away the taste of the plastic airline food and Mike was flagging down one of the ubiquitous state-owned taxis. It was an old American saloon of indeterminate vintage, and well battered, but its allegiance was marked by the pale green and white paint job.

Mike addressed the driver in Arabic, "kam hi al'ujrat 'iilaa alshaati fi khalij duda? What is the fare to the Beach of Douda? The driver's head went back in surprise then he recovered and began to consider what he should ask for the fare. It would be rude not to haggle.

"Hal takhudh dularat 'amrikiatan?" Do you take American Dollars? Mike knew this would hook him.
The driver's eyes lit up and he opened his mouth to speak...

Mike continued, "Eashrat dularat 'amrikiat 'iilaa shati duda. Watadhhab 'iilaa altariq almubashiri." Ten US Dollars to Beach Of Douda. And you go the direct road.

The driver had not made that much all week and just nodded happily. They climbed in and strapped up. The driver set off at a confident pace through the mixed traffic in the city centre then out by the Police academy to the East of town, then West on the RN2. Mac checked their route on his phone.

A mile and a half took them almost to a commercial dairy factory on the right of the road and here the driver pulled in to a well-used, if unofficial, lay-by. Mike handed him a 20 Dollar note and waved away his excessive thanks as they got out of the car. "Ashtari li'atfalik shyyan ma." Buy your children something.

Mac brought up a bearing on his phone, "Tha wadi ower there will tak us tae Douda. We need tae stick tae the right tae dodge the wummen-only beach. That wid get us banged up, even at this time ae night."

A couple of clicks over hard sand littered with rocks brought them to Douda beach which amounted to a couple of huts, a few thatched beach umbrellas and not much else. But there were a couple of people still at a beach bar even though it was supposed to close at 20:00.

"Bear left and we'll make the coast at the inlet of Douda Yar."

"Aye, Ah'll light up the beacon."

A minute after they arrived at the water's edge an unmarked Merlin HC4a came barrelling in at 180 miles per hour over the dead-calm sea. It rocked up and back on its rotor as it slowed and turned to land facing offshore, beside the kneeling men. They ran up the rear ramp and the Merlin was off the ground and back out to sea, closing the back door as she picked up speed before anyone could come to investigate the noise.

Mac gave the serious young crewman behind the side door gun a considering look, "Pal, ye'll no be needin' the chain gun the noo, Ah reckon."

19) <u>Tuesday 22:17</u> The RFA Fort Victoria
150 Miles South West Of Aden, Gulf Of Aden

The huge RFA Fort Victoria was making a modest 5 knots to maintain steerage way and counteract the roll as she ran East and West to maintain her position 150 miles off the coast of Aden, Yemen.

The Royal Fleet Auxiliary "replenishment oiler" was a marvel of engineering. Measuring nearly seven hundred feet in length, a hundred feet in width, and displacing over 31,000 tons, she was a behemoth, a giant that dwarfed the frigates that often accompanied her. But on this mission she travelled alone, pulled from a resupply task in the Indian Ocean.

Her onboard weaponry was significant; a formidable arsenal that included Phalanx radar-controlled chain guns, a couple of GAM-BO1 20mm guns she had held on to, and the ubiquitous Browning .50 calibre machine guns.

But these were merely for defence against the small fry of the sea; fast boat attacks. Her true strength lay in the three Merlin helicopters she housed in their comfortable hangars overlooking the Chinook-sized rear flight deck, two HC4a loaded for bear – or at least submarine. Each one a very real projection of power at sea. And a Mk4a to taxi the Royal Marines wherever they were needed. Effectively, she could make a circle of land or ocean a thousand miles across untenable for surface or subsurface vessels of any kind. And the Royals could do pretty much the same on land.

Despite her armaments, the Fort Victoria was not a combat ship. She was a fleet support vessel that carried the lifeblood of the fleet. Her cargo included 12,000 tonnes of heavy fuel oil, 120,000 cubic feet of ammunition, and 104,000 cubic meters of dry stores, ranging from food to replacement uniform buttons. She was the beating heart of the fleet, the ship that kept all the others at sea, enabling them to perform their duties, whatever in the world those might be.

And, of course, a compliment of Royal Marines ready for anything unexpected that might occur; from giving aid at a natural disaster to a rescue mission to all-out war at sea.

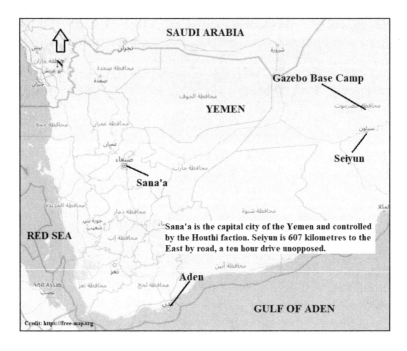

This evening was more pleasant for Captain Graham McLeod than some because he was not on the bridge, he was relaxing in his office with Mike and enjoying a glass of grog. It was such a pleasant change to have someone of equal rank to relax with and shoot the breeze, a naval Post Captain being equal in rank to an Army full Colonel.

"Can you tell me where you are going next Mike?" McLeod was being polite; he knew he had clearance and he knew he was going to be providing support to Mike as his orders had come in a couple of hours earlier.

"I'm not James Bond, Graham, we are just going in to Yemen to find that kidnapped doctor girl in the news. We have an agent amongst the locals, code-name Gravel…"

Graham interjected, "Sounds like *he* read too much James Bond…" Both men laughed.

Mike continued, "When I have my final orders in an hour or so I am going to cadge a lift from you and ask your people to drop us at an inland spot to be confirmed. We're going to meet up with Gravel, recce the place they are holding the girl, then plan an extraction. A team of SAS will be aboard you by that time and I imagine you will give them a lift out to us?"

Graham chuckled again, "Glad to be a help, Mike. Makes a change from running stores up and down the Gulf. Is your man sorted out?"

"He will have found the sergeants mess, that's petty officers for you isn't it? And he will be taking a *wee dram* with the Royal's Sergeant I would imagine." Mike impersonated Macs accent over the dram. Both men laughed in good nature.

20) Prisoner's Tent, Houthis Camp, Seiyun
Hadhramaut Valley, Yemen

Emily had not seen Rashid-Malik al-Houthi since she arrived. She remained fixed to the central tent pole but now on the end of a long chain attached to her wrist so she could reach a bucket. Over the last few hours she had discovered that there were two guards stationed outside the door flaps and they had looked in several times already. They seemed to be getting bolder.

The guards looked in again and this time walked into the tent and up to Emily, leering in the regulation manner. The uglier one reached out and stroked her cheek, she looked away. Then he squeezed her breast and she raised her knee sharply, catching him right on the money. He blew out the khat he was chewing and bent double in agony. The taller guard laughed like a drain.

Emily stood her ground and tensed for the reprisal but as the angry guard straightened up, death in his eyes, his partner restrained him with a hand, "yajib 'alaa tudhi almar'ati. 'iinaha 'akthar mimaa tastahiquh hayatina." You must not harm the woman yet, it is more than our lives are worth.

The angry guard's face turned to a sneer and spoke to Emily, "fi ghudun 'ayaam qalilat sawf yuetik rashid malik lana 'ajal sururina" Rashid-Malik will give you to us for our pleasure. His eyes suggested what might happen then.

21) <u>Tuesday 23:48</u> Merlin Mk4a Helicopter
19 Miles North of Seiyun, Hadhramaut Valley, Yemen

Fully kitted up, courtesy of the Royal's quartermaster, Mike and Mac rode in the back of a Merlin Mk4a with a net full of gear and a couple of quad-bikes slung below for quick release on site. There were three extra crew aboard, Royals who were to operate the side and rear door-guns, GPMGs, at their destination.

The Merlin left the Fort Victoria and flew East then North, gaining height to 15,000 feet and passing well South of Aden to cross the coast East of Al Mukalla. From there they flew North to a point some 19 Miles North of Seiyun, in the Hadhramaut Valley. Flying with no lights, the chopper spiralled down to 50 feet over broken ground by a pile of rocks which looked like a suitable spot to establish a base, Camp Gazebo as it would henceforth be known.

The Royals peered down their thermal gun-sights and the crew-proper kept a watch by thermal camera for life in the area. The under-slung load was lowered to the ground and Mac stepped out the door to grasp the cable stretching from the overhead winch-arm down into the darkness beneath them, "Weel, here goes sweet fuck all."

In seconds Mac and Mike were on the ground, Mike released the cable attached to the load net. The net sagged and the chopper climbed away.

They were alone behind enemy lines with no support within 300 miles.

Both men worked quickly to get their equipment hidden amongst the rocks before daylight.

22) Command Tent, Houthis Camp
Seiyun, Hadhramaut Valley, Yemen

Rashid-Malik al-Houthi sat at a folding table in his open-fronted command tent. The camp stretched away in front of him, a collection of tents visible mostly in silhouette by the electric lights set up on high posts around the camp perimeter and main walkways.

The night was warm and his young cousin Abdel sat companionably by his side. They had an ornate metal pot of coffee on the table and drank from tiny cups. Despite the late hour and the insects flying around them Rashid was smiling.

"Abdel, it has been good to see you again, my boy. Tomorrow we will.... Excuse me." Rashid took his 'phone from his pocket and checked the caller. It was Colonel Amir Tehrani. "What can he want at this time of night," he said to himself and pressed the button to accept the call.

"Rashid-Khan," Tehrani used the formal address for a leader of a tribe, "I hope this evening finds you well?"

"Colonel Tehrani, it is saved by your call. How may I be of service?"

"Rashid-Khan, our people have word that the British may be sending soldiers to rescue your guest."

"Colonel Tehrani, you are most kind to trouble yourself with this call; I am very grateful. I shall send out patrols to search for any unwanted visitors in this area."

"Rashid-Khan, you are wise beyond compare, as I have heard from all who know you. May Allah protect and guide you."

"Haji-Colonel Tehrani, may you rest in His embrace." Rashid ended the call having complemented Tehrani on his completion of an important pilgrimage. He thought for a moment then turned to Abdel, "We have work to do Abdel…"

23) <u>Wednesday 03:22</u> Gazebo Base Camp
19 Miles North of Seiyun, Hadhramaut Valley, Yemen

Mike and Mac had set up Gazebo base camp in just a couple of hours. The position was shielded on all sides by a collection of rocks sticking out of the valley floor, perhaps the remains of some long gone river island. This meant that on all sides they could see any approach over open ground; ground often referred to as a killing ground for the way in which it lacked cover and allowed approaching un-friendlies to be neutralised easily.

Their food, radio equipment and military gear were stacked in accessible piles and the pair of well silenced quad bikes were parked under some overhanging rock in case the Houthis or Iranians had brought some small drones to the party and chose to come looking around in their direction.

Mac had set a series of Claymore anti-personnel mines to cover strategic points where an assault of Gazebo might bottleneck; on tracks and between patches of rough-going.

Claymore mines themselves are like an 8 x 4 inch rectangle of plastic perhaps an inch and a half thick and curved over its longest side. Imagine your put a flat slab of plasticine over your thigh and bent it. This gives an outer and an inner flat side so upon the outer is marked, "Front, towards enemy" to help the hard of thinking.

In reality, the mine is a plastic-covered block of C-4 explosive with about 700 ball bearings set on the side to be pointed at the enemy and supported by four wire legs on one edge. As a rule the mine is placed where the enemy are expected to concentrate such as facing down a track or similar. When the charge is detonated, the blast wave does spread in all directions but the ball bearings are propelled at about 1,200 metres per second towards, hopefully, the enemy.

Claymores are devastatingly effective over a lateral arc of about 60 degrees and out to a range of 60 yards. At this range anything human or animal is reduced to finely chopped burger-meat. Out to 100 yards, nothing is going to walk away. Think of a huge shotgun, then make it bigger.

Mac completed what is always the final act in the ritual of setting up one or a hundred Claymores; arming them. The mine is detonated by an electric detonator called a "four finger det" for grisly reasons relating to what happens if they are held too long in warm hands.

He had already laid out the twin detonation wires from each mine to the firing point within camp and twisted both ends of each pair of wires to flatten any residual charge which might fire the detonator on connection. Then he visited each mine in turn and untwisted the det wire at that end and connected it to the two wires projecting from a detonator, keeping that item well away from the mine and his fingers in case of misunderstanding. Lastly, he slotted the detonator into a hole in the top of each mine and moved away.

This series of actions left him with the end of a pair of wires, twisted together and arriving at the firing point, for each armed mine. To fire any chosen mine from this point, its wires just had to be untwisted and touched to the terminals of a battery. A battery which was kept with its terminals carefully covered.

Mike watched him arm each mine from the firing position through night vision goggles. Mac had worked through the slightly tiresome ritual steadily and methodically without rushing or cutting corners and finally came back to join him. "I always get tense when I see someone arm a Claymore," were Mike's first words.

"Aye, me too, pal. Aince seen a detonator blow when the squaddie didnae twist the wires first. Just some leftover current in the wires was enough."

"I sent a message to the local James Bond, Gravel, via London. See if he is up at this time."

"He's likely cozied up in bed wi' a local lassie."

The satellite 'phone shook quietly and a green light flashed. Mike pressed a button to take the message, "Talk of the Devil."

The message marched along the tiny screen, "Gravel will arrive your loc 07:00 Local Time."

"Fancy."

"Aye."

24) Command Tent, Houthis Camp, Seiyun
Hadhramaut Valley, Yemen

The rising sun had painted the sky a ridiculous vivid pink over the mountains to the East of his camp and the dawn found Rashid-Malik al-Houthi haranguing his barber, Asif. The small, bald and much-put-upon man of no important family said nothing but continued to trim Rashid's thick beard carefully, then apply scented oils, all the while subjected to a rant which ranged in subject matter from his training in a college for the blind to the effect of the camel genetics in his lineage.

Wiping away the excess oil with a hot towel Asif stood back, head bent and hands clasped in front of his crotch. Rashid stood and walked away then turned and paced back across the tent in obvious agitation. He walked over to the radio and called up Colonel Amir Tehrani. After the obligatory, but brief, exchange of pleasantries he cut to the chase, " Colonel Tehrani, I am concerned that the British are hidden and evading our search patrols. My heart would beat easier if you had brought your elite forces to support our meagre strength here."

There was a pause as Tehrani was slightly taken aback by the uncouth paring-back of the appropriate etiquette, "Rashid-Khan, my cousin, even now my men are gathering to equip an armed column which will drive to your location with all speed. Though my men are not to be spoken of in the same breath as your desert warriors, they will be sufficient to take responsibility for our guest and escort her safely back to Iran by way of Sana'a."

25) Wednesday 06:55 Gazebo Base Camp
19 Miles North of Seiyun, Hadhramaut Valley, Yemen

Following the age-old British Army custom, the two men had stood-to, manned their chosen fighting positions, at Gazebo from before dawn and would have remained until the sun rose a little higher yet. Since time immemorial the enemy have attacked at dawn or sunset more often than any other time and it made sense to be ready based purely on the odds.

Given the open ground around the camp, Mike was behind a medium range, semi-automatic sharp-shooter's rifle with a high rate of accurate fire, the LMT LM308MWS Sharpshooter.

Probably the most effective sniper rifle in the world at the time was the Accuracy International L115A3 bolt-action "long range rifle" chambered for the .338 Lapua Magnum (8.59mm) round and good for 1.5 mile kills. But this, like all sniper rifles, had a slow rate of fire due to the manual bolt action and was rather a delicate animal to keep zeroed.

Some people are not aware that a tap on the barrel of a sniper rifle, let alone on the sighting mechanism, will ruin the alignment between sights and bullet-path rendering it useless until it is zeroed once more by firing a group of rounds at a clear, small target a set distance away. Not a convenient task during a fire fight.

As a result of the Generals in command of armies traditionally preparing to fight their last war again, pretty much all modern infantry soldiers are armed with some variation of an assault rifle for the urban warfare expected in a European conflict against, this time, the Russians. In essence, this is a conveniently short, light-weight weapon firing light-weight ammunition for ease of carry and producing a high rate of fire, to suppress enemy fire quickly, but accurate only over very short distances as a result of all these choices; particularly the light-weight .223 round.

When the Western armies went to Afghanistan they found that they were fighting in more open ground than was usual in Europe and against an enemy who often had older weapons with a greater accurate range. This sometimes led to the uncomfortable situation where a Western unit was surrounded by an enemy too far away to shoot but who could shoot them if they showed themselves.

Of course there were sniper teams in the Western forces, and they were employed widely and successfully, but owing to the limitations of mobility brought about by weight, rate of fire and delicacy of construction, they could not accompany a rifle section on patrol. So there was seen to be a need for some kind of weapon which fell between the assault rifle and the sniper rifle in terms of ruggedness and effective range. The result of this line of thought was the "sharp-shooter." Both the name of a rifle-type and the designation of the one or two men armed with that rifle and assigned to each infantry section.

The Sharp-shooter-weapon was a rifle with a more rugged constructions, a higher, semi-automatic rate of fire to support the section, and a longer range to take out enemy unreachable by assault rifles, something in the region of 800 yards. As a happy compromise, the sharpshooter rifle was designed and chambered to take the heavier 7.62 x 51 round, the same as the GPMG/M60, so the availability of ammunition already supplied for machine guns was not an issue.

Mac had a Sharpshooter rifle by his side but his attention was focussed on his collection of detonation wires running out towards most of the likely avenues of approach to their position. A rifle fired at night tells the world where you are from the flash and will get you shot at. A rifle fired in the day will produce a puff of smoke if the cleaning oil is not well wiped away; but a hand grenade or a command detonated mine gives no clue as to your whereabouts and for this reason they are very popular amongst seasoned, and therefore cynical, soldiers.

As might seem obvious, the two men were facing in opposite directions as they covered their arcs of responsibility. For this reason Mac was the first to see the bobbing motion of an approaching head coming into view over cover at a distance. A head covered by a red and white keffiyeh tied in the Yemeni way like a turban and without the agal band often worn by Saudis.

Mac tapped the but of his rifle with the fingers of his hand to attract Mike's attention and then stretched his head in the direction of the approaching individual. He could now be seen to be mounted on a camel, seated in the traditional Yemeni way, so who was he? Carefully, Mac selected the pair of wires which led to the Claymore covering the man's approach. Mike scanned the middle distance around the camp through the telescopic sights on his rifle for anyone else moving, or perhaps trying to hide as this scout moved forward.

As the rider approached more closely, the light brown shal became visible draped over his left shoulder, an identifier given by Gravel to mark him out. Mike saw it first and clicked his fingers then made a palm down, side-to-side gesture which Mac understood to mean, "Don't kill him." But they remained wary until the man picked up a stone and placed it on a rock at the edge of camp. An agreed action so harmless, yet unique, that it proved his identity beyond any reasonable doubt. Unless Gravel had been captured and tortured overnight, of course.

26) Airbus A220-100, 3 Miles S of The RFA Fort Victoria
50 Miles SW Of Aden, Gulf Of Aden

E Squadron, 22 SAS are an elite within an elite. They are the squadron of the Special Air Service which is tasked with supporting British intelligence operators, usually MI5 or MI6 people, when they require close protection in the UK, when they are working in unfriendly parts of the world, or when they are in need of other close military support.

Despite their reputation for ruthless efficiency in combat, it is a prerequisite of E Squadron membership that a chap should be capable of blending into the background of an apparently civilian setting. So they should at least look civilised; and this requirement has ruled out some of the more fearsome looking characters in the regiment such as the one who could hold a house-brick in one hand and break it with his other fist. Though not the one who could somersault over a man's head from standing. By comparison, most of E Squadron looked fairly normal.

Mac was still a member of E Squadron, and a well-liked one, despite his semi-permanent attachment as bodyguard to Colonel Mike Reaper of MI6. And his mates were coming to support him.

The Airbus A220-100 had been flying all night from Bristol Airport, UK in the confident expectation of Mike having found the hostage and come up with a plan to free or kill her. It was assumed that 8 men would be quite sufficient. Now the aircraft was approaching a spot 3 miles South of the RFA Victoria, she having steamed some way closer to the seat of the action, 50 miles South of Aden.

As with so many things in life, this aircraft was not quite what it appeared to be. On long charter to the British Ministry Of Defence, it was used to transport up to a hundred fully armed troops wherever they were required at short notice. A facility called upon more regularly than some might imagine. It was painted in radar-absorbent material so that it would not be noticed overflying most sensitive targets.

With a cruising speed at 40,000 feet of 550 miles per hour and a range in excess of 4,000 miles the RAF A-220 had covered the 3,400 mile trip to RAF Akrotiri, refuelled and flown the last 1,750 miles South to the Victoria in one hop leaving plenty of fuel remaining to get back to Akrotiri without mid-air refuelling.

Now the pilot, Squadron Leader Andrew Henderson, was considering where he would have to switch his transponder back on before landed again in Cyprus.

It its current configuration, the A-220 had one row of seats running down each side of the fuselage as this left plenty of room for equipment and extra men could always sit on the floor. This morning there was no need for discomfort as there were only nine passengers, Captain Oliver Beaumont-Blackwood and his eight men, together with the usual three airmen of the dispatch crew.

The aircraft had been descending gently for a while and Henderson had one eye on the altitude meter. "There, levelling off at 10,000. Tell our guests we are at altitude and will be in position in minutes 15, Martin."

"Wilco, sir."

In the back the RAF jumpmaster nodded to the SAS Officer and the soldiers stood to check their gear. In 15 minutes they would jump at 10,000 feet and steer their Ram-air chutes to land on the back deck of the Victoria. For men as proficient as these, and with 'chutes capable of a 5:1 glide ratio, landing on the football pitch sized chopper pad on the aft deck of the Victoria was a walk in the park.

27) <u>Wednesday 09:11</u> Gazebo Base Camp
19 Miles North of Seiyun, Hadhramaut Valley, Yemen
The three men sat cross-legged around a solid-fuel stove which had just produced three mugs of strong, sweet tea. The smell of coffee, while wonderful for moral, carries too well to be tactical.

Gravel had introduced himself as David Bradley and came across as the expected product of the English public school system; clever, educated, cultured and well socialised. As one might expect of an MI6 field operator. He continued, "… So I took a look around their camp, its just on the edge of Seiyun actually, and could see no obvious sign of her."

"How did ye ken she wis in their camp?" Mac asked the question on his and Mike's minds.

"That is what I got from London. They told me they believed she was being held at Seiyun by Rashid-Malik al-Houthi's bunch of cut-throats." David looked to the two men in turn apparently slightly puzzled at their interest in this detail. His response had seemed comfortable and honest, but was it?

"David, I am taking what you say as being true," A flash of concern ran across David's face, "but we stay alive by checking every little detail. Much as I suppose you have to." David nodded his head, as if he understood.

"The thing is, it seems to me rather strange that London know exactly where she is. Or think they do.

David thought for a moment, "I did wonder about that myself. It is not impossible that we have either an agent or an informer inside Rashid's outfit."

"Would you know, David? I guess you couldn't know?"

"I would have no idea. Need-to-know and all that."

 "I wondered about that myself," Mike thought aloud, "And when you are dealing with an Arab tribe like the Houthis, different rules apply than to Europeans. MI5 had the IRA riddled with informers and agents because the leadership were a bunch of thugs pretending to be patriots and therefore they were open to bribery. Its not like that with Arabs. This is all about belief and family. They are notoriously difficult to corrupt and impossible to infiltrate."

"Fair assessment, I would say."

"So I dismissed the idea of an informer as unlikely. But not impossible."

"Obviously," David went on, "You can't plant an agent in a family organisation like that but you can sometimes play on rivalries and jealousies. And sometimes blackmail. I have heard of it being done."

Mike nodded, "Yes, I thought the same."

"At the end ae the day it makes nae odds. We ken where she is an' she cannae help hersel' or us tae get her oot."

The other two looked at Mac. With an unerring sense of timing, a green light began to flash silently on the their comms device. "That'll be the angel Gabriel wantin' a blether."

Mike pressed a series of keys and a map of their location and the surrounding area appeared on the small screen. Superimposed on the map was a jagged line of red glowing points off to the West of their position. This was a warning from the drone circling high above them and watching the area with infra red and other sensors for the approach of potential enemy forces. "That looks like an enemy patrol to me, guys. If it were our support they would be marked in green. And any civvies going about their business would be in single file on a track, not extended line. Lets see if we can get a visual."

The three men picked up their rifles, David's being an almost comically older Lee Enfield .303, and they climbed up the rock selected by Mac as the activation point for the Claymore because it offered a good view. This time of the morning the sun was quite low and it lit the scene from behind them to provide excellent visibility while leaving their ledge in shadow.

After a moment, a movement could be seen out at 200 yards near where the sensor had shown. Then it was gone and another appeared. Trained soldiers were approaching by the alternate movement technique where half move while the other half hold position in cover ready to give suppressing fire.

Mac looked to Mike who shook his head. "Give them time to get closer. Chances are they only think we are here and have not made a contact report to their HQ. I want to make sure we get them all so that doesn't happen. And I want to do it quietly so we will leave the mines in reserve and break out the MP5 SDs."

"I'll grab one fur Dave here." Mac moved off quickly and quietly to their weapons store.

"Are you familiar with an MP5 David?"

"Yes, though I have never used one in combat."

"But you have been in a fire-fight before?"

"I've used my pistol in anger several times if that is what you mean."

"I just wanted to check you were not a virgin." Mike laughed and both men knew he was referring to the hesitancy some men feel before their first kill. "You see the rock by itself, over there?"

"Yep."

Mac arrived and silently handed David a silenced MP5 SD with six full magazines.

"I want you to take a position high up on that rock, South of the enemy, and try not to show yourself. When you see me take my first shot, kill any of the enemy that you can see. Do not change your position until you get my signal."

"I understand." David was serious but did not seem unduly nervous, more workmanlike.

Mike nodded in the direction of the enemy's North side. Mac rocked his head back in understanding, "I'll tak the ither flank an' we can mak a tidy job ae it."

The two ran off to their positions, bent from the waist, partly from the need to avoid being seen by the enemy. Mike settled down into his firing position and got comfortable. A sub-machine gun firing 9mm rounds is accurate to 100 yards with a little care and this contact was going to be just inside that.

The broken cover and rough ground did not make for a neat formal advance and the leading edge of the enemy had broken its line-abreast. The South side was more in advance and passing David's position before the other side reached Mac's front. Mike waited, judging the moment. He aimed and squeezed the trigger, dropping a man in the centre of the enemy formation with one shot. Probably no one else noticed amongst the enemy as the bullet was sub-sonic and the suppressor first class. But David and Mac were watching closely and began firing themselves.

The men of the enemy patrol only realised they were been shot at when six of their number were dead. The remaining five men looked around wildly for their assailants, not sure where to hide. The correct response to being caught in an ambush is to charge the enemy, on the basis that a properly set up ambush has a killing ground behind the victims so they cannot run to safety and very probably has mines set up in any places suitable to take cover.

For this reason, a charge gives the best chance of survival, albeit a small one, and at least charging the enemy gives the ambushees something to occupy themselves with in their last moments.

The Brits continued to fire steadily and in less than eight seconds all the enemy were dead. A slow kill rate, as in most ambushes the enemy are dead in 2 or 3 seconds, but this was the single shots of a few ambushers against a larger enemy unit.

"We'd best get the bodies unner some rocks. This place has vultures like we get sparrows back hame."

28) Prisoner's Tent, Houthis Camp
Seiyun Hadhramaut Valley, Yemen

The taller guard led the shorter through the tent flaps. Emily noticed a look in their eyes that betrayed a shared joke. They walked around her and looked her up and down like prospective camel buyers. Emily had time to feel uneasy before the short one spoke to her in broken English, "Rashid-Malik al-Houthi has captured you, unbeliever, and therefore you are his property to do with as he will."

Emily looked down to avoid the men's eyes.
The tall one continued the one-sided conversation, "He has said that he will give you to us for our pleasure." Both men leered as if they were in a Victorian melodrama.

"Thuma ealayk 'an tuqarir man minkum sayahzaa bi li'ana 'iietayiy lirajulayn Haram" Then you must decide between you who will have me, because to give me to two men is Haram. (Forbidden)

"Madha taerif ean alharam 'ayuha alkafir?" What do you know of Haram, infidel? The guard was angry but puzzled and now cautious.

"'Aelam 'anah la yajuz li'ahad minkuma 'an yalmisani hataa tantahi dawrati li'ana dhalik harami." I know that neither of you may touch me until I have had my cycle as that would be Haram.

Both guards stared at Emily. She continued, calmly, "Waean 'abi saeid alkhadrii qal: qal alnabiu salaa allah ealayh wasalam fi 'asraa 'awtas: <<la tuqarib hamil hataa tadeu, wlan ghayr hamila>> hataa tahid maratan wahidatan. wahadha alhadith sahahah alshaykh al'albaniu fi 'iirwa' aljalil"

"Abu Sa'eed al-Khudri said: The Prophet (peace and blessings of Allah be upon him) said, concerning the prisoners of Awtaas: "Do not have intercourse with a pregnant woman until she gives birth, or with one who is not pregnant until she has menstruated once. This hadeeth was classed as saheeh (Authentic) by Shaykh al-Albaani in Irwa' al-Ghaleel"

The guards stared.

"Wa'aelam 'aniy sa'uqadim li'iiran hadiatan min rashid malik alhuthi kama hu min haqihi. hadha sayajealuni jariatan lil'iimam wasataerif ma euqubat tadnis 'iihdaa sariaat al'iimami? sayatimu dafnuk muntasiban ealaa ktifayk warajman bialhijarat alsaghirat hataa almawti."

"And I know that I am to be given to Iran as a gift by Rashid-Malik al-Houthi as is his right. This will make me a concubine of the Imam and you will know what the punishment is for defiling a concubine of the Imam? You will be buried upright to your shoulders and stoned with small stones until death." In Shia Islam, as followed by the Houthis and Iranians, the Imam is not just one of many religious teachers but the single, infallible leader in all matters somewhat like the Roman Catholic Pope.

**29) <u>Wednesday 11:47</u> Merlin Mk 4a Helicopter
21 Miles North of Seiyun, Hadhramaut Valley, Yemen**

After a thermal imaging scan had shown the area to be clear of both humans and goats for some miles around, the Merlin spiralled down from 15,000 feet to stay within the cleared zone.

After hovering briefly at 30 feet to release the grounded net of quad motorcycles the chopper moved to the side a few yards and touched the ground briefly to allow 9 men to leap out of the side and rear doors. These men immediately formed an outward-facing protective circle by laying prone around the aircraft until it took off and climbed steeply into the clear sky.

As the helicopter rose into the dark sky Captain Oliver Beaumont-Blackwood stood and checked his electronic navigation aid for a bearing; then for easy reference took note of the silhouette of a distant hill which lay on that bearing. Meanwhile the men had cleared the netting from the quads, hidden it under bushes and begun freeing the machines from the frames which protected them in transit.

A couple of minutes and the 6 quads were lined up behind Oliver and purring very, very quietly through their silencers. Like a photogenic US cavalry officer, Oliver waved them to follow him and led off along a wadi which ran in roughly the right direction.

**30) Command Tent, Houthis Camp
Seiyun, Hadhramaut Valley, Yemen**

Rashid-Malik al-Houthi was studying a report from his quartermaster which suggested that his command was eating more than the local town. He was interrupted by an obviously troubled young officer. "Sir, the patrol covering the Northern approach has not returned and cannot be contacted on the radio."

Rashid looked at the young man for a while as he thought, his fingers pulling his shiny, black beard gently. "I believe we have visitors on the way, Imran. Strengthen the guard and make sure they are aware that there is an enemy approaching."

Imran made a half bow, "Immediately, sir," and ran off.

Rashid picked up the radio handset and looked at it for a moment before using the pressel. He asked the operator on Colonel Tehrani's callsign to put the Colonel on. A few moments passed then, "Rashid-Kahn, may a blessing be upon your house. What may I do for you?"

"May peace be upon yours Colonel Tehrani. I believe we may have a British force approaching our position to rescue the girl. I would value the support of your forces."

"What have you seen of them?"

"One of my patrols seeking intruders has disappeared completely and without any trace overnight."

"Then we know nothing other than there is likely a force approaching. I passed Marib an hour ago and will be with you tonight, if Allah wills it."

**31) <u>Wednesday 12:33</u> Gazebo Base Camp
19 Miles North of Seiyun, Hadhramaut Valley, Yemen**
It had been discovered that Gravel was a past-master at making tea in just the way that British soldiers like it: Hot, lots of dried milk-powder and so much sugar that they can almost stand the spoon up. All the men were supplied with a mug of this brew and sat or lay in various relaxed poses around the map which Mike had laid on the floor.

In some units even today it is normal for the officers alone to be briefed for a mission but in the SAS, SBS, Royals and airborne forces it is assumed that all the men are capable of working on their own initiative in case of separation or disaster, so they all need to know the big picture and sit in. Briefings are still carried out in correct form though. Mike scanned the attentive faces...

"**Ground:** The Houthis Camp we will be dealing with is made up of a dozen tents with no obvious hard points, trenches or even sandbagged emplacements. The ground between here and there is pretty much the same as you saw on your way here. There are roads into the Houthi Camp from the East and West and a couple of towns too far out to make any odds.

Situation: The Houthis are a tribe, a big family really, plus hangers-on. They are led by the head of the family who is a youngish man we know little about. They are not trained soldiers, more an armed gang that runs a protection racket and are trying to go national. For religious and political reasons, the Iranians support them.

There is a young English lady, a medical doctor no less, kidnapped and held captive by the leader of the Houthis in his tented camp on the North side of Seiyun. It is likely the Iranians plan to fly her back to Iran and hold her hostage against the release of the tanker full of Iranian oil recently seized by our sailor boys.

Mission: Our job is to release this young lady and get her back to the Victoria. If we cannot release her we are to kill her. Under no circumstances must the opposition be allowed to transport her away from here because they will take her to Iran and use her as a bargaining tool.

At 03:00 in the morning we will hit their camp from two sides at 90 degrees as marked on your devices, catch them in crossfire and eliminate them. Team Alpha will then enter the camp and bring out the girl while Team Bravo remains in position in case of a counter attack or other interdiction. When we have the girl we will ride back to here for extraction by Merlin.

Enemy Forces: We believe this Houthi chap has forty or fifty experienced fighters in his camp. His men are not well trained by any standard but they can shoot. All the locals can shoot. But we also understand that there is a strong detachment of Iranian Special Forces on their way to collect our young lady as we speak. We should be in and out before they arrive but, as those of you who have dealt with them before will know, they are pretty handy soldiers. Well led, well trained, well equipped and aggressive.

Attachments: We have the facilities of the Victoria on call. In practice that means the Merlins and anything they can carry. There is also an MQ-9A Reaper drone on call. Flying out of Saudi should things get sticky.

Command and Control: When we are in position, my shot will be the signal to open fire. When the enemy are suppressed, I will take Alpha into the camp and secure the girl. If anything happens to me then Captain Beaumont-Blackwood will take over and complete the mission.

Signals: All signals and frequencies are listed on your devices together with the route plan.

Any questions gentlemen? Is there anything I have not thought of before I tell London we are going ahead?"

32) Royal Air Force Station Waddington, Lincolnshire, UK

Squadron Leader William Naseby sat comfortably in a gaming chair, a chair which was in a metal box something like a shipping container, itself within a large shed at Royal Air Force Station Waddington, Lincolnshire, in the East of England. The box was actually a fairly comfortable, mobile control room for flying Reaper or Protector drones launched from anywhere in the world.

Squadron Leaders only fly drones when they want to; such as interesting special missions for the secret squirrels. William relaxed and settled a little more comfortably into the chair. His eyes flickered left and right, bouncing from his weapons operator to his intel man. He had told them to get some sleep as they were pulling a double shift.

Easing his back, William adjusted his headset and looked casually at the screen giving the flight stats of the MQ-9A Reaper drone he was flying. It was operating out of King Khalid air base in Southern Saudi Arabia near the city of Abha and he was patrolling the main roads between Sana'a and Seiyun at an altitude of 20,000 feet in the hope of recognising and stopping any reinforcements reaching the Houthi camp.

On his aircraft's bomb struts were 2 Laser JDAMs, laser guided bombs of 500 pounds apiece. Each of these bombs was capable, being of the newer type with pre-fragmented casing, of killing everything within an area of about 4 or 5 acres when detonating

over open ground. It was also carrying four Hellfire II anti-armour missiles which could be guided either by radar, camera or thermal imaging camera during darkness.

An indicator began to flash red on his screen marking a potential target. William instantly shook himself alert and his crew were awake before he touched the screen to zoom in and bring a convoy of more than a dozen military vehicles into view. The radar had automatically locked onto the centre vehicle in the group and the AI was waiting for him to make a decision regarding an attack.

33) <u>Wednesday 19:03</u> Colonel Tehrani's Special Forces Convoy East Of Marib, Yemen

Colonel Tehrani rode in the third vehicle of his convoy. His idea being, first not to be in a vehicle blown up by an IED (Improvised Explosive Device) on the road ahead, and second that should the unit be ambushed he would be close enough to the centre of his unit to command the survivors efficiently.

To make best speed the IED detection unit on point were running 100 yards ahead of the column and taking risks. Behind Tehrani, A Pantsir-S2 missile launcher on a KAMAZ-6560 8×8 truck followed his vehicle. Behind this, its wide-range radar support. Realistic air cover was a necessity now with US and Saudi drones lurking behind almost every cloud.

The lead vehicle slowed down to a crawl, as did the convoy behind it.

The night was clear and bright but the men were all keeping their eyes wide open as they drove through wild country Eastwards towards Seiyun. If it was true that Rashid's patrol had been hit there was every chance of a drone attack or an ambush and every man in this elite unit was tense. And ready.

In the radar truck the sergeant reacted to the buzzing alarm instantly and called the officer commanding the Pantsir (Carapace), "Incoming radar lock! Target 15,000 feet, 2 miles bearing 178 degrees."

The head-set replied instantly, "Target seen!"

In the KAMAZ-6560 the Captain had already seen the target on his guidance radio and his sergeant had pressed the button to initiate the firing sequence. Because of the high altitude of the target the AI left the guns inactive and instead armed a pair of missiles. The first fired in a couple of seconds, locked onto the target by radar.

From behind the vehicle cab the missile screamed into the sky leaving a thick trail visible in the truck lights. A couple of seconds and it was supersonic. The missile Captain was taking no chances, "Fire again," he ordered and a second missile was away to bring the odds of a kill from over 70% to a near certainty.

He could have saved a missile as, high above them, the first missile struck the MQ-9A Reaper drone and destroyed it utterly.

Tehrani half smiled in appreciation of the crew's smooth operation and, presumably, his own survival. He picked up the radio handset again and spoke to the IED team, "The chances of there being an IED between us and Seiyun have risen significantly, so take every care necessary to find it."

34) <u>Thursday 02:52</u> Prisoner's Tent, Houthis Camp
Seiyun, Hadhramaut Valley, Yemen

Emily lay on a camp-bed, like the other women in the darkness of the tent. The one difference in their condition was that she was tethered to the central pole by a long thin chain to her wrist. It was locked in place, held around her slender wrist, by a small padlock.

Her wrist-watch had been stolen, of course, so she had no accurate way to tell the time. The Isha prayer, last of the day's five prayers and held after full dark, had been called by the muezzin many hours ago. During her confinement she had listened for the changing of the guards and counted them. It seemed they were doing 4 hour stags and changing at 18:00, 22:00, 02:00 and 06:00 so far as she could tell.

The 02:00 change had occurred and the same two guards were on duty with whom she had had the unpleasant interactions on the previous days. Somehow she was pleased about that. She couldn't see the Big Dipper constellation and tell the time from that, but there was a gap where the tent flap met the top edge of the doorway and this had created a just-visible moon-shadow on the tent wall opposite. She had taken close notice of where this fell at the 02:00 guard change yesterday and where it was by the 06:00 change.

By estimation of the shadow's travel she saw it must be a little before 03:00 and she must not be late. She managed to work up some saliva in her mouth and spit it onto her wrist. It was a poor fastening anyway and the chain loop came over her small hand without too much trouble. Doubtless they never imagined she would try to free herself. Without attracting the attention of the other women, she tensed and relaxed her whole body a number of times to get the blood flowing and her slender frame ready for action.

She began to make a quiet keening sound. A little louder. The shorter guard put his head in the tent doorway and she continued. He came in and leaned over her, close enough for her to smell his breath. His mistake was that he held his rifle in both hands across his front but he left his Jambia, his wide, curved dagger, unguarded. Emily snatched it by the handle and drove its 3 inch wide blade horizontally into his chest to slip between his ribs and make a wide wound in his heart. He was dead before his body slumped onto her.

Dropping the knife, Emily picked up his AK47 and pulled back the cocking lever to half-open the breach and check the state of the weapon. It had a round in the chamber ready to fire, an amateur habit for someone on guard duty but convenient in that she would not have to make the noise of cocking it. She detached the magazine and depressed the top round to check it was full. It was.

He had a couple of full magazines on his person and she stuffed these down the front of her shirt. A glance under the fore-stock showed the weapon was not of the Chinese type with an attached, folding bayonet so she found the bayonet in its scabbard on the corpse and quietly clicked it into place.

Looking around the room she saw a pair of frightened, staring eyes showing a woman to be awake but keeping quiet. Good. Emily began to make a moaning noise. A noise which might make a man think she was having sex. She moved to the side of the doorway and waited a few seconds until the shorter guard came hurrying through.

By the time he was a yard into the dark tent his back was exposed to her and she pushed the bayonet into his rear left quarter above the kidneys. His body arched back and she twisted the rifle, using the magazine as a lever, to turn the bayonet inside his body and make a huge and quickly fatal wound. As he fell to the floor the bayonet came out of his back with a twist of intestine turned around it. Ignoring this decoration she plunged the bayonet into his back, higher up this time to find the heart.

The two Arab women were now both awake and staring at Emily in silent, wide-eyed horror. One held her hands over the eyes of her daughter. Emily looked from one to the other, "Wayajuz qatl almughtasib dfaeaan ean aleifati." It is permitted to kill a rapist in defence of one's chastity.

Then, outside, all Hell broke loose.

35) <u>Thursday 03:00</u> Outside The Houthis Camp
Seiyun, Hadhramaut Valley, Yemen

Captain Beaumont-Blackwood had led Bravo Team to the top of a collection of boulders just to the East of, and overlooking the Houthi Camp. The men had taken up fire positions with good views of the tents below. Geordie was on the GPMG and Chalky, a Fijian Islander, was beside him as his number two and gun-crew commander. Chalky was laying out the lengths of ammunition belts he had collected from the other men to supply the gun, "What sort of dick head put their camp under the shadow of this bloody great rock do you think?"

Geordie said nothing. He was known for speaking as if he were paying for the words.

"It's going to be shooting fish in a bloody barrel. They've even set up a ring of lights so we can see what we are doing! I feel sorry for the bastards down there. Almost. Still, makes for a quick in and out..." Chalky stopped because Geordie looked as if he was going to say something.

"Aye. Canny, though." (Yes, but a good situation for us to be in.)

Chalky waited in case his mate had anything to add. No that was it, "Looks like the Colonel is in position."

"Aye."

"Make sure you don't touch that tent in the middle, there."

"I seen it."

Alpha Team was in position on the North side of the camp so both teams could fire into it without shooting at each other. One rifle opened up with a short burst, then an instant later the rest of Alpha Team, then the whole of Bravo Team.

Geordie was steady and methodical in all he did. In his shooting he was no different and fired a 4-5 second burst into each tent in turn. With a cool gun, and the gas regulator wound back correctly, that was around 50 rounds per burst. Ridiculously fast as covering fire but ideal for this murder-job. Each burst riddled a tent, sufficient to leave nothing alive. Four tents and the belt was out so Geordie lifted the top cover and Chalky laid in the new belt. Cover down, pull the working parts back, rinse and repeat.

All the men had head sets to the radio net and a call came over, "All stations Bravo, Alpha Niner, Switch fire now over."

The Captain replied for his team, "Bravo Niner Switching fire now out." He looked to his men who mostly made eye contact and nodded. Chalky tapped Geordie on the shoulder, "Aye." Geordie switched his aim high above the camp and continued firing to keep the enemy's heads down as Alpha Team stormed the camp.

Inside the camp there were no targets. One or two men dead on the floor. The six men of Alpha Team quickly checked the interiors of the outlying tents for any threats then approached the central tent, weapons raised for instant use. The tent flap opened and Emily stepped out, AK47 held down by her side to show no threat. A length of intestine still hung from the saw edge on the spine of the old Type II bayonet. Seeing Mike she tucked a wayward strand of hair back behind her ear in a strangely feminine fashion, given the circumstances.

"Emily?" Mike shouted. More a statement than a question.

Emily nodded, "I'm Emily Cooper… Colonel." As she saw the rank insignia worn on the buttonhole to his shirt.

"I'm glad we didn't frighten you… Doctor," Mike was as dry as the sand.

36) Command Tent, Houthis Camp
Seiyun, Hadhramaut Valley, Yemen

Rashid-Malik al-Houthi lay on the floor of his tent, a bullet wound in his lower leg and another through his chest which had broken a rib and caused his left lung to collapse. He was hidden behind the corpses of two of his men who had been about to relieve the perimeter guard. In his hand,

Rashid held the microphone to his radio at the full extent of the cord. "Colonel Tehrani, can you hear me. It is Rashid," he said in breach of all good radio security procedure and coughed up blood.

Someone on the radio in Colonel Tehrani's unit must have been quick on the uptake and fetched the Colonel, "Tehrani send, over."

"This is Rashid-Malik al-Houthi. My camp has been overrun by the British and the captive taken. All my men are dead…"

The radio was quiet for a few moments. Then the Colonel began to speak as if to an old friend, "Rashid-Khan, this is Tehrani. I hear you. I will arrive at your camp in just a few minutes. And I will avenge you…"

37) Northern Perimeter, Houthis Camp
Seiyun, Hadhramaut Valley, Yemen
A little more than 50 yards outside the Houthis camp the British soldiers were converging on their quads accompanied by Emily. The signaller fired up the comms to Fort Victoria and called in a sitrep, "Hello Goliath, this is Foxbat, over."

"Goliath send over."

" Foxbat. The goose is in the oven. ETA extraction loc figures four zero, over."

The reply was almost relieved, "Goliath copy that. Out."

The sound of heavy trucks could now be heard off to the West of the Camp.

"Let's make a move guys." Mike led off on his quad heading back to Gazebo, Emily riding pillion with her AK47 supported comfortably on her hip as if she was in a Mad Max movie.

38) <u>Thursday 03:18</u> Western Perimeter, Houthis Camp
Seiyun, Hadhramaut Valley, Yemen
Colonel Tehrani's convoy arrived at the edge of the Houthi camp and the combat units spread out in line abreast North to South. They advanced and reached the camp, the infantry advancing ahead in pairs. Tehrani reached the command tent and saw Rashid on the floor, still alive, "Medic! Help Rashid-Khan." Then to his lieutenant, "Search all the tents for wounded and get them treatment. Have a sweep made of the camp perimeter and

find out which way the enemy left. I expect it will be to the North but confirm that."

"Yes, Colonel."

Tehrani stood in thought for a moment then strode off back to the vehicles. He found the Special Forces Captain he was obviously looking for, "Put together a strong motorised pursuit team and move it to the North side of camp ready to chase down the attackers when we have word of their direction."

"Yes, Colonel."

A call came into his headset over the local net, "Charlie Niner, Charlie 3 Niner, there are light vehicle tracks leading away to the North. They appear to be on a number of quad motorcycles. Over."

39) North Of Houthis Camp
Seiyun, Hadhramaut Valley, Yemen

Mike pulled his quad off to the side of the track and Mac stopped by him. He waved the men past until the Captain reached him, "I expect the Iranians will come after us within minutes so take Dr Emily and get her back to Gazebo. I will sort out something to slow down the pursuit."

"Yes, sir."

Emily climbed up behind the Captain and all the quads left bar Mac's.

"Claymores aye?"

"Claymores, aye." Mike replied, dryly. Without another word the two men produced a pair of the mines from their panniers and set them up staggered and pointing back along the track to catch the maximum number of pursuers. Mac rigged up a standard trip wire across the track a foot off the ground and some way back towards the Houthi camp. A few seconds fiddling with wire and the mechanism was set: A pull on the tripwire would fire a four-finger detonator taped to two lengths of detonation cord, one leading to the detonator in each mine. The Claymores would then fire and mince anyone on or near the track for a distance of about 80 yards.

Det cord is a "cord" of high explosive used for the rapid transmission of a detonation pulse from one detonator or explosive charge to another. Looking very much like off-white washing line, it has been disguised as such in an insurgency situation.

Det cord consists of a plastic wrapper around a core of Pentaerythritol tetranitrate (PETN) and has a VOD (Velocity Of Detonation) or "burn rate" of a little over 6,000 metres per second. In this case, therefore, it would set off the mines a couple of milliseconds after the first detonator was triggered.

The two men the rode off after their comrades.

40) North Of Houthis Camp
Seiyun, Hadhramaut Valley, Yemen

The chase was led by a dozen off-road motorcycles, each with a pillion passenger, and they were drawing ahead of the light vehicles carrying Colonel Tehrani and most of the men when they reached the trip wire.

The effect was nothing like it appears on TV. There were two, almost instantaneous, flashes and two sharp cracks as the mines detonated. The 1400 ball bearings travelled in two close swarms at a speed of 1,200 metres per second; about the same velocity as a high-power rifle bullet.

And each ball bearing had very much the same effect as a bullet. So the eleven leading riders and pillions were cut to pieces, along with their mounts. The lead three motorcycles burst into flame as the fuel from their riddled tanks was ignited by the hot blast-wave from the mines.

Colonel Tehrani pulled up short of the kill-zone, head and shoulders out of his vehicle and spoke to a sergeant in the next vehicle, "Deploy an infantry screen ahead on either side of the track to check for any more surprises sergeant."

"Yes, Colonel."

41) The RFA Fort Victoria
30 Miles Off Al Mukalla, Gulf Of Aden

Below the water level and behind the bridge is the armoured heart of the Victoria; the Operations Room from where all activities aboard and off-ship are controlled and coordinated. It is much like the Ops Room on a Destroyer but much bigger, with more than a dozen seats for ratings behind radar screens, cameras, radios and much more technical equipment; plus room for officers to discuss their plans and options while maintaining contact with the eyes, ears and hands of the ship.

The Captain of the Royal Marines detachment, Richard Blakey, turned to address the Captain, "They have neutralised the camp at Seiyun and collected the hostage. Beginning their return to Gazebo, sir."

"Very good Captain." Then turning to the Flight Officer the Captain of the ship said, "Have a Merlin on immediate standby for an extraction please."

The petty officer on the secure satellite comms system followed protocol by addressing the officer in charge of his section, "Sir, message for the Captain from Flag on secure."

That officer looked to repeat this to the Captain, as per protocol, but he was already at the screen and reading, "Kraken to Goliath: MQ-9 Reaper Drone supporting your people has been taken down by the Iranians. This strongly suggests they have at least medium anti-aircraft capability and that your Merlins are at risk."

The Captain turned to the officer, "Send message received." He stroked his beard and began to pace beside the briefing table. "So," He said to the Executive Officer, "it appears we are not going to be able to get our people out."

42) <u>Thursday 05:24</u> Gazebo Base Camp
19 Miles North of Seiyun, Hadhramaut Valley, Yemen

Mike and Mac raced their quads back to Gazebo and through the gap in the rocks which led to an area sheltered from observation. Captain Oliver Beaumont-Blackwood met them, his men already being deployed to defensive fire positions. Mac went to find a brew of tea and Mike spoke to the Captain, "They are probably ten minutes behind us, Oli.

"Mmm, not ideal. Victoria signalled they cannot do an extraction with choppers owing to the Iranian's having strong anti-air. Seems the Reaper Drone sent to slow them down was taken out last night."

"That is awkward. Do they have any Jackals on the Victoria?"

"Couldn't say, Mike. They might have a jumbo jet hidden in one of the store-rooms. The boat's like a city."

"I will have a word with the Victoria." Mike began to move away.

Oli held his hand to the ear-piece on his headset, "Wait…"

Mike stopped.

"Our recce drone crew say the Iranians have arrived and deployed to cover all sides of the camp. Motorised equipment is still moving around. Looks like a battery of heavy mortars."

"Probably their knock-off NATO 120s. Tell your men to dig shell scrapes against the mortars. And take care moving around as they will all have night-vision."

"I imagine they will begin with the mortars any time soon, don't you think?"

"Any time now, they don't need the light." Mike moved off now.

"Bugger." Oli shared every veteran's distaste for being bombed by heavy mortars.

There was a crack from high up on the rocks as an SAS sharpshooter took out a target of opportunity.

Mike found the SAS signaller under a rock overhang, busy scraping out a hollow with a folding shovel. "Open a call to the Captain of the Victoria, please." The man nodded wordlessly to Mike and spoke into his Stenomask-type microphone. After a few moments he seemed satisfied and handed it to Mike.

"Goliath, Sunray. We probably don't have much more than 1 hour before we are overrun. I am looking for an extraction but understand the opposition have anti-air effective against Merlin. Confirm all, over."

"Goliath, Confirm that, over."

"Sunray. We have laser target designation here. Do you have anything to carry munitions? Over."

"Goliath. We do but there are three MQ-9d Protectors en route to you from Saudi. Should be there in an hour. Loaded with Martlets."

"Sunray. Many thanks. Out." Mike checked his watch to work out the Protectors' ETA and grimaced.

Mac arrived by Mike's side with a steaming brew in each hand. "They're too faur oot tae dae much 'cept the odd pot-shot wi' a lang-rifle."

"They will be making a final assault when they think they have softened us up enough with the mortars. Save your Claymores for that. Dig out the

Ghost (Ghost Drone 6) and set the PLFs (Pulse Repetition Frequency) for Martlets."

"Aye. Drink yer brew."

Six deep thuds came from the middle distance in three sets of two. Someone shouted, "Incoming." Someone else replied, "Thank you."

Mac shook his head, "Tha's one-twenty mortars, Ah reckon. Three tubes. Bedding the base-plates in so they are set up already."

Another shot from a heavy calibre rifle high up.

The six 120 mm mortar bombs landed in a rough grouping just outside the camp.

"Could dae better."

The signaller called to Mike, "Boss!"

Mike walked over, and the signaller explained, incredulous, "They are asking us to surrender, boss."

Taking the microphone from his hand, mike dropped the voice procedure, "Hello Iranian commander, this is the officer commanding the rescue unit."

There was quiet for a moment, then in perfect, rather friendly, English, "Hello commander, I am Colonel Tehrani of the Iranian special forces. We have you surrounded and have cut off your escape by air. You must surrender or I shall have to kill all your men. You will, of course, be treated with the respect due to prisoners of war."

"Hello Colonel Tehrani, I am Colonel Anderson of the Coldstream Guards. It is an honour to make your acquaintance. I am afraid I cannot accept your offer. Without wishing to sound like our American cousins, you will have to take my rifle from my cold, dead hands. And I wish you good luck with that."

"Very well then, Colonel, I would expect nothing less. Good luck to you too. Goodbye."

Three more deep thuds came from the same direction as previously.

"Rangin' shots."

A few moments of silence passed then there were three terrific explosions, deafening and dazzling in the half light, as the 120 mm mortar bombs detonated inside the perimeter. Two on the ground and one high on a rock. The hail of shrapnel whistled over the heads of the men laid in their shell scrapes.

One of the troopers chuckled in relief, "They only have point detonating fuses!" He was referring to the fact, obvious now to everyone there, that if the Iranians had the ability, they would have set their mortar bomb fuses to burst in the air above the shell scrapes and thereby do a lot more damage. The next minute passed in a haze of deafening explosions, dazzling flashes and whistling shrapnel as twenty four more bombs rained down onto their position in quick succession.

Captain Beaumont-Blackwood quoted Macbeth, calmly, "Life's but a walking shadow; a poor player, that struts and frets his hour upon the stage, and then is heard no more: it is a tale told by an idiot, full of sound and fury, signifying nothing."

Someone said, "Well a miserable Jock would say that, wouldn't they?" There was a laugh from the audience, the usual response to weak military humour.

"Fuck off all o' ye." Mac rolled over and behind the little screen showing the area covered by his Claymores. "They're on their feet, boss." He selected a pair of wires marked with two tape tags and held them by a battery, ready.

Two shots rang out from higher up amongst the rocks.

Captain Beaumont-Blackwood caught Mike's eye, "Mortars?" Mike nodded and the Captain looked to his mortar teams, now ready behind a pair of 60 mm mortars. Using a set of pegs driven into the ground a couple of yards from each tube they began to fire onto pre-ranged points as quickly as they could drop bombs down the tubes; turning them as they went to spread their fire across the Iranian infantry now out in the open and approaching Gazebo.

Mike watched his screen and saw a number of the enemy soldiers cut down; the remainder retreated or took cover. "Mortars cease fire. Back in your holes please, gentlemen."

All the men returned to their shell-scrapes and another dozen mortar bombs fell amongst them. Someone shouted, "Medic! Staffy's been hit." Then another, "Medic!" Emily crawled out of her shell-scrape and tore the field dressing from a wounded man's rifle butt then bound it to staunch the bleeding from a jagged shrapnel wound across his thigh.

The Captain was watching his screen, "Here they come again. Mortars! Return fire please." The mortar teams began raining their small bombs, set to air-burst, on the approaching Iranians. Again a number went down, but this time they made the edge of the rocks surrounding the camp. The troopers began to use their rifles.

Mike shouted across to the Captain, "Looks like they mean it this time. Have your men hold the perimeter with rifles and mortars, I will see where our support is." The rifle fire increased, unasked.

The SAS mortar teams continued to fire at a more leisurely pace and the first of Mac's Claymores detonated with a sharp crack. He spoke into his microphone, "Goliath, Sunray, give me an ETA for Protectors, over."

Sunray, Goliath, ETA less than minutes figures 1, over."

Sunray, copy, out." "Mac, put someone on your Claymores and take over the Target Designation, please."

"Wilco, boss." Mac clicked his fingers at one of the troopers who crawled over to take his place at the Claymore wires without a word. Mac then crawled over to that man's shell-scrape where there was a small screen and a control box, something like a video game controller.

43) 20,000 Feet Over Gazebo Base Camp
19 Miles North of Seiyun, Hadhramaut Valley, Yemen
High above Gazebo a flight of three radar-invisible MQ-9D Protector drones arrived on-scene and began to circle like robotic vultures. Imagine a Reaper Drone that can carry over 2 tons of bombs or missiles, fly for more than 2 days, see a mouse in the dark from 5 miles up, work as a team with other drones and think for itself…

44) Gazebo Base Camp
19 Miles North of Seiyun, Hadhramaut Valley, Yemen
Mac lay on his belly in the shell scrape and made himself comfortable. In front of his face, the Ghost Drone 9 control screen showed an ariel view of the Iranian positions. For a few seconds he typed into the console, jabbing

with his index fingers but deftly for all that. "Partnership established," came up on the screen and he muttered at the machine, "Well that's awfy friendly ae them."

He set the Ghost to bank and twist autonomously, all the while keeping its cameras locked onto the area he had selected. This way he was not relying on the plastic body and rotor, or the high refractive index, radar-absorbent coating to avoid the Iranian radar. It took a few moments to make out the mortar tubes and he placed a cursor over one of the three. Then he selected options to order, "Target this and all similar targets within given area. Fire at will."

20,000 feet above him one of the Protectors considered it's options for a millisecond and switches clicked in three of the Martlet air-to-ground missiles on its bomb racks. The first stages fired, they accelerated ahead of the drone and turned downwards sharply. Then the second stage motors lit up to accelerate them to twice the speed of sound as they dived towards the Iranian mortar positions.

A little less than 9 seconds later the Martlets had covered the almost 4 mile decent and detonated 10 feet above each of the 3 mortar positions, killing their crews and destroying the mortar sighting equipment.

Mac was already laying the cursor onto the anti-aircraft missile launcher. This time he told the lead Protector, "Target this and all vehicles within given area. Fire at will."

Milliseconds later, lots of switches clicked in the bomb racks under all three Protectors.

45) Ralf Burgin's Office, SIS headquarters
85 Albert Embankment, Vauxhall Cross, London, UK

The view from his penthouse office at SIS headquarters on 85 Albert Embankment Vauxhall Cross was breathtaking; overlooking the busy River Thames with Vauxhall Bridge to the left and, opposite, the city's age-old buildings and towering new skyscrapers. Here, ensconced in an opulent office adorned with classical furniture and the finest art, sat Ralf Burgin. To be fair to him, he was almost as big a player as he thought he was.

Ralf looked up from his desk as the door swung open, and his sharp eyes met Mike's intense blue gaze. Mike's lean and athletic figure stood blocking the doorway for a moment as he habitually scanned the room for threats before entering and making for the seat opposite Ralf.

A pretty girl poked her head around the door in response to Ralf's hidden signal and smiled a question. "Tea for two please Joanna."

"Still in one piece then, Mike?" The question was both a statement and a friendly greeting.

"My luck is still holding for the moment," Mike continued the light theme. "Dr Cooper was not all she seemed then, was she?"

Ralf was on the spot but replied smoothly, "It seems not," he began, implying ignorance, "But if I had known she was one of ours I couldn't have said. You know that."

"Of course not, Ralf, I wouldn't want to know who she was and then be persuaded to blow her cover on an Iranian operating table." On cue the door opened and the young lady entered bearing the tea sacrament.

46) The Royal Opera House, Covent Garden, London UK

Mike had chosen Covent Garden Opera house for their first date because, in his experience, girls liked to be taken somewhere they could wear a nice outfit. And Bizet's Carmen because it had lots of songs you could hum along to.

More to the point, the central character was a women of spirit, very much like Emily in some ways, so she might appreciate that; take it as a compliment if the parallel was subtly brought to her attention.

He sat in the foyer of the Opera House, behind a tepid coffee at a table by a window through which he could see the pedestrian approach from the tube station. A strikingly beautiful girl was walking towards the entrance, head up, shoulders back; she stood out from the crowd like she was under a spot light. Surely that was not Emily? He stood and made for the door to meet her, catching the eye of the barista who had already formed the impression he was on a hot date. She smiled encouragement.

Emily stepped into the foyer looking like an entirely different woman to the one he had seen just a few days earlier, dressed then in baggy rags and patching up the wounded. Tonight, under a faux-fur coat, a long sparkly gown over a tall, slim figure and a black choker with a jewel of some kind to set off her lightly tanned, and now he noticed it, unusually beautiful face; then up to her dark hair piled high on her head. She looked like a princess.

"Very nice," he thought to himself.

If you enjoyed this book please give it a 5 star review on Amazon and you will help more people get to read it.

Best wishes from Robert and all the team at Military Press.

Cap badge of The Palace Security Group

The next book in the series is…

Kill or Capture – An SAS / MI6 Mission

When an undercover MI5 operator vanishes from inside a drug gang, Colonel Mike Reaper, MI6's smartest operative and his fearsome Scottish/Glaswegian SAS bodyguard Sergeant "Don Mac" MacLeish, are thrown into a desperate hunt for the source of a deadly drug-cutting additive. Their search takes them on a breakneck global odyssey across three continents:

In their latest adventure they are battling drug cartel soldiers in Columbia and Russian special forces in Lagos, Nigeria.
This story features all the fancy SF kit and tactics you would expect from Dalcross so buckle up for:

- A deadly fire-fight against Colombian drug cartel soldiers
- Covert insertions by HAHO parachute and submarine
- A harrowing descent into the underbelly of Lagos, Nigeria, where Don Mac is captured by ruthless enemy forces
- A heart-stopping SAS raid to snatch crucial evidence from a heavily fortified base

This is a pulse-pounding thriller for fans of Robert Ludlum, Tom Clancy, Lee Child, LT Ryan, Dan Brown and James Herbert. Its packed with intrigue, danger, high-tech weaponry and cutting-edge SAS combat skills.

Visit www.robertdalcross.com for access to further maps and photos.

Warning: This book is about 4 times as long as Extraction Under fire.

Read Kill or Capture today!

Available from Amazon in paper and electric